Taking A CHANCE At Love

Taking A Chance At Love

BY

KESHA PRIDE

Published by

Pride Books

Pearland, TX 77584

ISBN 978-0-615-41078-4

Printed in the United States of America

AUTHOR'S NOTE

This book is a work of fiction. Names, characters, places and incidents either are the
product of the author's imagination or are used fictitiously, and any resemblance to actual
persons, businesses, establishments, events, or institutions is entirely coincidental.

ACKNOWLEDGEMENTS

There were so many people that helped me through this development, whether it was directly or indirectly. There were those that showed support like P.Diddy, TM, and BNB.

Then there were those that went above and beyond. Ntense, thank you for your many hours spent listening to me vent; for contributing your poetry; and for providing feedback when asked. Stacy thank you for all the advice regarding publishing, the book cover, and marketing. You helped to make this possible and encouraged me when I got frustrated. You brought me back to focus when my mind would bounce from idea to idea and task to task. And most of all, to Kimmy Kaze, without you, this would not have been possible. You helped me mold the characters and storyline by reading each chapter and providing feedback and critique. Your assistance is so profoundly appreciated. Thank you, Brittny "Ruby Dee" Mandarino, for your poetry contribution.

A special "Thank you" goes out to Jackson of Amuse Bouche Entertainment who created my book cover. You are blessed with such an amazing talent. You took my story and put it into pictures. You dealt with my indecisiveness and showed patience when I changed my ideas over and over and over again. I look forward to working with you again in the future.

When I started writing this story, I had no plans of sharing this outside of my circle of friends. But Jackson invited me to an event called HeArt & Soul in Houston. It was a meeting of the creative minds and those who loved to surround themselves with art. It is a place "where the arts merge." It was amazing to see so many talented people right here in good 'ole Houston.

As the story grew, I fell in love with my characters and felt like their story needed to be shared to as many people as would read it. After visiting HeArt & Soul, I decided to make my contribution to the artistic world. I hope each of you enjoys it as much as I enjoyed creating. Sit back, relax, and enjoy as you step into the pages and live the story.

Thank You,

Kesha Pride

FOREWORD

Without a Strap

I fucked her without a strap.
Yet, I penetrated her with my pussy
And my eyes.
Thrusting her hips against my hips,
Her wetness spread from her toes,
To my fingertips.
I could taste her pleasure.
I fucked her without a strap.
Yet, I touched spots an
Eight-inch "cock" couldn't rock.
Instead, my fingers ran deep
And her white 'dialect'
Had an ironic twist of a French accent
If heard with virgin ears.
But still, her words made sense to me.
I fucked her without a strap.
Yet, my caress was simply explicit
In ways to illicit a side of me that's been hidden.
She fucked ME without a strap.
Yet, her words
Flowed across my skin
Like coffee touching my lips,
The back of my throat,
With each sip,
My thoughts,
My body,
Would dip deeper and deeper and deeper into her.
But when I DID fuck her with a strap,
She arched her back
And well...
That's a different story.

-- *Ntense*

INTRODUCTION

"It's hard to wait around for something that you know might not happen, but it's even harder to give up when you know it's everything you ever wanted." ---- Unknown Author

I could not have put it into better words. As humans, we tend to shy away from -- even be afraid of -- the unknown. From a personal standpoint, I am a planner. I hate surprises and I prefer for things to go as I imagined. Unfortunately, or fortunately -- depends on how you look at it -- when you are talking about love and relationships, you have to deal with the unknown. However, how do you make sacrifices for a relationship that may fail? How do you give your all for something that's not guaranteed?

Webster defines love as a "feeling of strong attachment induced by that which delights or commands admiration." The Urban Dictionary describes love as "the most spectacular, indescribable, deep euphoric feeling for someone." Several other dictionaries give similar definitions. The thing they have in common is a strong feeling towards someone else. There is no mention that love only has to exist when it is returned. I love someone. She means so much to me. Love is either there, or it isn't. And with her, it's there. I truly love her. I fought it. I tried to play hard like I didn't have those feelings. I even tried to convince myself that it was lust or infatuation because it happened so soon. But it's still there. I acted out, tried to push her away, and sabotaged the relationship at times. But it's still there. I don't know if our love will last but I know that I love her regardless.

There are people that try to keep us apart. People so set on us not being together that they will threaten our lives. But our biggest hindrance is our careers. We aren't permitted to love each other. She said to me, "Why does it matter what you are giving up if you are giving it up for something you really want more than anything else?" For once, I was speechless. That really hit home. What are sacrifices if ultimately I get what I truly desire? Maybe I can't be as open with my relationship as I wanted to be. Or maybe I even have to maneuver the system and bend the rules to make the relationship work. But these are all small sacrifices if it's for the thing I really wanted, which is forever love and happiness.

The thing is, it's not guaranteed. I could make all the sacrifices aforementioned and still end up alone. People gamble money everyday.

Money that comes and goes but is needed to survive. But we are afraid to take chances for our future. Isn't it time we do all we can for the chance at love?

For all the overachievers, career-minded, professional, ambitious women out there: We give our all everyday for our jobs and our education. Why couldn't we do the same for love? For the strong, independent women: We have fought and done so much for ourselves to get us where we are. Why couldn't we do the same for love? For the proud and the confident: We show our self-assured exterior on a daily basis, yet we hesitate to show our softness, vulnerability and sincere emotions. Why can't we hold our heads high and show our love?

For the chance at love, I will give freely of my affection and myself. For the chance at love, I will submit myself to the moment. For the chance at love, I will make sacrifices both material and symbolic. For the chance at love, I will wait around for what might not happen because otherwise I might be walking away from everything I ever wanted.

1

CHAPTER ONE

Tori

I hear the birds chirping and cars driving by. The sunlight is arranged across my bed in streaky patterns through the cracks of the faux wood blinds. *Why on earth did I decide to live in the city with all this vehicular and foot traffic?* Even through the closed window I could smell fresh cinnamon rolls and cookies being made in the bakery across the street. *Ugh! It's too early in the morning.*

The sheets next to me rustle and my legs are assaulted ---- no, strike that ---- my legs are caressed by soft long legs as the creature sharing my space stirs. I pretend to be still asleep as I feel her prop up on her elbow, watching me. Her finger lovingly traces my face from my ear, to my jaw line, to the outline of my lips. Still pretending, I whimper softly, licking my lips, in my 'sleep'. This encourages her. I feel the bed shifting and my heart picks up the pace. Her moist lips connect with mine. Still 'sleeping,' I whisper incoherently and turn my head slightly towards the window, away from her.

She laughed her feminine, flirty laugh and says, "Girl, get up. I know you are *not* sleeping. We both know you wouldn't turn your head towards that window with all that sunlight coming in like that. First thing we need to do today is get some dark drapes to block that sun out of my baby's eye in the morning. You are like a vampire. And then we need to unpack some of these boxes and do some grocery shopping. And you know the movers are coming this afternoon. Baby, I hope they remember the special instructions we gave because if the elevator . . ." Her next words were muffled as I kiss her firmly and passionately. I had sat straight up and watched patiently as she presented her early morning speech and with each spoken word, her pink tongue called to me. I pulled her head to mine and claimed her mouth and tongue.

I felt her heart beat increase in speed and intensity as she straddled me. The beat of hers, matching the beat of mine. I grab her long dark brown hair and massage her scalp with my fingers. She loves when I do that. I feel her grinding her pelvis against mine as she tries to ease the fire we've ignited. "Slow down baby," I whisper as I reluctantly break the kiss. I flip her over on her back and straddle her. My hands caressing her breasts as my lips and tongue make licking and sucking motions across her neck and lips. They make the journey following my hands, down to her breast, across her flat stomach, down one thigh, and up the next.

She shudders as I near her hot spot. Her moans and whimpers drown out the sounds of the birds. Her sweet scent eliminates the smells of the bakery across the street. And the vision of her anticipatory facial expression makes me forget about the sunlight that was annoying me minutes ago. Now that sunlight is my friend as it bathed across her beautiful caramel brown skin and face. Unable to hold out any longer, I dive in to feast on her . . .

"Good morning Atlanta! This is Rainbow Skye waking you up in the morning on 103.1, home of the Rainbow Skye Morning show." The sound of the radio alarm pulls me out of yet another perfect dream. "This is ridiculous!" I screamed to the empty room, as I yanked back the covers I had become tangled in during the night. My feet touched the cool wood floors and I scowled at the sunlight pouring

through the windows. I looked around, seeing the boxes around the loft's master bedroom.

I shook my head when I realized I *was* smelling cinnamon rolls and cookies from the bakery across the street. My stomach growled with impatient demand. I frowned at the sounds of the birds and the many cars driving by. As I look over to the space next to me, I am disappointed to see an empty space, even though I knew there was no one there when I went to bed last night. I grunted my disappointment but pushed those thoughts away as I remember where I am.

"On our show this morning, we are discussing this Van Der Sloot character and his role in Natalee Holloway's disappearance. This little boy has some nerve. Five years after Holloway's disappearance, he kills another woman. Yes, I said another, because I do believe he killed Holloway. I mean, the boy confessed, people. Authorities said his confession made no sense. That the story did not fit their suspicions. What type of nonsense is that? If he was stupid enough to confess, whether or not the story was true, he should be convicted, if only on the basis of stupidity alone. But we'll discuss this and much more later on in our show. Right now, I want you to get up and get your day

started right with the Rainbow Skye Morning show on 103.1, WVYU, The View."

My name is Tori and I am a new resident of Atlanta, Georgia. I am so new, most of my belongings are still in transit from Houston, Texas. I made it in last night and knew right away, I would need some drapes on the floor to ceiling windows. I am not a morning person and sunlight is not my friend. Not until I have had my shower, anyway.

I am twenty-nine years old; two weeks shy of my thirtieth birthday. Believe me, I am not looking forward to it. That milestone is the reason for all these painfully pleasant dreams. Growing up, I set goals for myself. I wanted to finish my bachelor's degree at twenty-one. Medical school by twenty-five. Residency by twenty-nine. And become partner in a practice by thirty-five. I have been able to accomplish it all. I even became partner in a small anesthesiology group here in Atlanta and I still have five years and two weeks to spare. I have been blessed. But the one thing I wanted more than anything else was to be happily in love. Married, even.

Of course, back when I was playing with dolls and riding bikes, my idea of marriage was different that it is now. Then, I was going to marry a doctor. A tall, dark, and handsome man with dark brown eyes, pearly white teeth, and curly black hair. Let's just say I am looking at life through different eyes. My idea of a life commitment now is meeting a beautiful, professional woman. I want a wife. A life partner. I want children but I don't want to *have* children. Yes, people. I am a lesbian. A lesbian who wanted to be settled by the time she turned thirty.

So at the age of twenty-nine-going-on-thirty, I am struggling with the notion of being single at thirty. It's not like I'm fat or ugly. In fact, to brag a bit, I am quite the beauty. I stand at 5'6 and weigh 145 pounds most of which is toned arms and legs and a round butt. I have a slim waist with very toned abs and a small (but not flat) chest. I turn heads in dress clothes or scrubs. I have had my share of female attention but just haven't met 'the right one.'

There have been a few times, especially after I turned twenty-four, when I thought I had met 'the one.' But after a few months of bliss, these women showed their true colors and had me running for the hills.

I, myself, have broken a few hearts. There were some who met all my physical criteria but when it came to brains, they were seriously lacking. My friends say I am too picky. Maybe I am, but I want to be able to have mentally stimulating conversation with my mate. Nothing turns me on like a woman with a degree and some sense to match.

So when the sexy chic with the banging body has no idea what my job entails, or what the housing market disaster means to homeowners, or how to calculate the sales price at a 30% off sale, I bail. And I do mean bail.

My numbers change, I block you from my Facebook and Twitter accounts as well as my Skype and Yahoo Chat! What can I say? I hate confrontation. And these women did not like the idea of losing out on their 'doctor'. Especially the ones who felt like I was their ticket out of the hood or their momma's house.

It took a lot of energy but I finally dragged myself out of bed thinking about this latest dream. I actually saw her face this time. I've had similar dreams but none so vivid and definitely none where I saw her face. And what a beautiful face it was. The almond shaped, dark brown eyes, perfectly shaped nose, pouty lips, and smooth jaw line. I couldn't help but smile at the image.

Snapping back to the here and now, my smile fades when I realize, *I have no idea where my overnight bag is in all this chaos*. I had moved a few things over from Houston a few weeks earlier. Things the movers refused to handle themselves. Boxes and artwork were everywhere. I flew in late last night and put my overnight bag around here, somewhere. *AH HAH!* There it is, across the living room. *How did I make it to my room last night anyway?*

All the boxes scattered haphazardly throughout the space made the two bedroom loft style condo seem closed in and small. It will look even smaller when the movers arrive with my other things later. The private practice group I am joining has included a two-year lease in this midtown high-rise condo as part of my contract. What a blessing that was.

You see, I am fresh out of my medical fellowship where I made just enough to survive. I had no idea how I would manage to relocate, find a nice place to live, and still manage to eat. But when this group in Atlanta recruited me, they put their best offer on the table, and man, was it good! I received multiple offers from practices across the country and one other in Atlanta.

Atlanta was appealing to me because of its reputation of being one of the largest gay cities as well as the "Black Mecca." The thought of being surrounded by my people (African-American and the gay family) was enough to make my decision. So when Sleep Tight Anesthesiology presented their package with $300,000 base salary, private office with computer, minimal call shifts, and this awesome condo in the heart of the nightlife, I signed the two-year contract and packed my things. Sure, it was hard leaving my family and friends in Houston, but I could always get a cheap ticket back home or they can come here. It was time for me to step out on my own.

I was born and raised in Houston, Texas. I completed my undergraduate degree at Texas Southern University, a HBCU, and my medical degree at Houston Medical College. I stayed on and completed my residency and fellowship at the hospitals in Houston. I had been there all my life and was ready for a new scene.

The day I opened the contract from Sleep Tight, my mother and stepfather took me to the dealership to buy me my first new car. I felt guilty looking at cars at the Mercedes dealership because I *thought* my parents didn't have much so why should I use their money to splurge on a new car. Well, it turns out, my parents -- I call my stepfather "dad" because I didn't meet my biological father and until medical school, never knew my stepfather didn't give me the other half of my DNA -- had saved quite a bit of money in their retirement.

We never really spoke about my family's finances. I just assumed that since we'd been living in the same house since I was five that that was all we could afford. My mom was a schoolteacher in the Houston Independent School

District and my father worked as a sanitation employee –
garbage man – for years until he was named director of
Harris County Waste Management. They'd saved up a
chunk of change by remaining in our small home and were
now making plans to travel during their retirement.

My biological father left me a substantial amount of
money in a trust that I was able to acquire once I completed
my medical training. He did so in his will. He died my
second year in medical school. I never knew about the
trust, or him, until he passed and even then, I had no clue as
to the amount of money I would get. Apparently, 'daddy'
had made some wise decisions in life. At least, financially.
Lord knows, his decision to leave my mother while she was
pregnant with me, was not a smart decision on his part. My
mother was as good a woman as any man – or woman –
could get. She was determined, strong, and loyal. She took
care of home even while working overtime, tutoring out of
the house. It was definitely his loss. But he never had any
other children so he left all his money to me through the
education trust and in his will.

So this morning, I am looking forward to my new car
being delivered as well as the other items the movers
loaded up from my old apartment in Houston. My mom
told me to donate all that stuff and buy new furniture once I

got to Atlanta, but I am not used to having money yet and was a bit leery about spending it. Although, now I am looking at this huge contemporary space and wondering how my '90s black leather couch with the tape on the arms would fit in. *Maybe I should make a trip to the furniture store. Tomorrow. Today, I have to shower, head to the office to sign employment paperwork and meet the rest of the team, and then meet the movers back here.*

I turned the volume on the bedside clock radio up so I could hear Miss Rainbow Skye as I showered. She had such a sexy voice and from what I've seen in some local ads, she looked just as sexy. I hope I got the chance to meet her one-day.

I dressed in a hurry, brushing my hair back into a neat ponytail. There was no time for straightening it out with the flat iron. Checking myself in the bathroom mirror, I was satisfied with my appearance. I made my way to the garage elevators. The garage was underneath the high-rise building.

I boarded the elevator and as the doors began to close I saw a hand slip quickly between the doors causing them to reopen, revealing an unbelievably sexy woman in a sports bra type athletic top and running shorts. Emerging from those shorts were long shapely legs. She was a runner, for sure. She stood about my height, maybe an inch taller, and had the shapeliest ass I had ever seen, except for on the strippers back home. Her breasts were perky and round in the athletic top. Her almond shaped eyes were sparkling as she caught me staring at her.

I looked away hastily but continued to observe her out of the corner of my eye. Her caramel colored skin was smooth and silky looking. Her black-brown, relaxed hair was pulled loosely into a ponytail and her face was free of any evidence of make-up. Yet, she was breathtakingly beautiful.

She took in my attire. Androgynous dress slacks, button down tailored shirt, and dress shoes. I wanted to be comfortable today. I wasn't big on dresses. Barely wore them, actually. But at that moment, I wish I had worn a sexy skirt and revealing blouse. She didn't seem to approve of my attire as she turned to face the door.

"Good morning," she said as she reached in front of me to push the CLOSE DOORS button.

"Good morning," was my timid response. We remained quiet until the elevator came to a stop at the basement level garage. She stepped out of the elevator with me following. I notice we were parked three spots apart in the assigned lot. She was getting in her car when she turned to me and said, "Guess we're neighbors. See you around, handsome."

OMG! Wow. Not only did she speak to me, she flirted with me. *And she called me handsome. Which means she thinks I'm a stud. Or at least, I think that's what she meant.* Except, I'm not really a stud; *although I've been called that a time or two after some late night bedroom romping.* Should I correct her? Should I go introduce myself? *Is she gay, bi, or just playing with me?*

Before I could answer any of my own or ask her any questions, her black Mercedes S63 AMG pulled out of the parking garage, squealing as she exited. Shaking my head, I smiled. My Mercedes S63 AMG will be here this afternoon. Mine is silver. *I hope she doesn't think I tried to copy her.* After all, this morning I am driving the rental car company's Chevy Impala, and this evening, I will have the same vehicle she has. *This ought to be interesting.*

2

CHAPTER TWO

Kenya

I looked out the driver side window at the hot, but obviously shy woman. I loved that she admired me but respected me at the same time. Her smile was warm and seemed genuine. When I first stepped into the elevator, I could feel her confidence stirring around me. Until I 'caught' her staring, that is. Once she realized that I noticed her noticing me, she became timorous, almost uncomfortable. I knew she was gay by her attire, the way she looked at me, and the ring. She wore that symbol on her left thumb, proudly. I wish I could be that bold. But I was bold in other ways. Like how I unabashedly flirted with her.

Looking back, I probably shouldn't have done that. She is my neighbor. What if she had flirted back? What if she came knocking on my door expecting a follow-through? *That is too close for comfort.* Besides, I am focused on getting this next year out of the way so I can really pursue my dreams. I had no time for quick flings or romantic entanglements.

My name is Kenyatta Jackson but everyone calls me Kenya. I am twenty-eight years old and I am a doctor. A surgeon. Well actually, I am finishing up my surgery fellowship at a local hospital in Atlanta; following in my father's footsteps. Don't get me wrong, I've always wanted to be a doctor, but I would have been content being a pediatrician. My father convinced me that surgery would be more thrilling and rewarding and to be honest, he was right. I absolutely LOVE my job.

I am a true southern belle. My mother is from Lafayette, Louisiana and my father from Memphis, Tennessee. They met when both were attending Morris Brown College, in Atlanta. My mother is a college professor at Atlanta University and my father is a neurosurgeon. I am an only child and most people can tell. I just say I am blessed.

That blessing seemed to disappear when it came to my love life. I had the absolute worse luck with relationships. I haven't had a real girlfriend since undergrad and that lasted just thirteen months. Since then I have had quite a few flings that I somehow miscalculated as more.

I've dated nurses, teachers, lawyers, and graduate students. The one thing they all have in common is their drive. I cannot date a lazy woman. There's just too much I want in life and a lazy person would just hold me back.

The exception to that prerequisite was with my one and only lesbian relationship. I dated a girl I went to college with. We met at a club and exchanged numbers. I found out, during our first conversation, she and I went to the same school. In fact, we were in the same math class. Her name was Skye. It was so unique and so was she.

Skye was a journalism major with hopes of having her own TV talk show "like Oprah." She was fascinated with Oprah's wealth more than her talent. At first, our relationship was just about sex because I had never considered having a serious relationship with a woman. But then Skye and I started doing other things together. Art shows. Open mic nights. Movies and independent film showings. It was great. She worked nights so we didn't spend many *nights* together but it didn't bother me because she said she was doing an internship at a local TV station which could be an opening for her dream.

One night, a few of my friends invited me out to the strip club to celebrate one of the girls' birthday. We were having a great time watching the dancers and even receiving a few lap dances. It was my first time going to that club and I was having a blast. I almost felt guilty for having that much fun without Skye.

The DJ announced the next set and a dancer by the name of Rainbow. The guys, who I assumed were regulars, started cheering rambunctiously. A few were at the stage before the dancer even came out. When she finally made her appearance, the crowd went wild. There were cheers and catcalls as she did tricks and made her booty pop.

As I got up to use the restroom, I passed by the stage and decided to tip the dancer that was hanging upside down on the pole only by the strength of her arms. She circled the pole, easing her way to the floor. Then I saw the familiar tattoo on her breast and looked straight into the eyes of Skye.

I was stunned. I returned to the table, grabbed my purse telling my friends I was not feeling well, and drove home. I didn't hear from Skye until the next day when she came knocking on my door. She was so nonchalant about the whole thing, saying someone had to pay her bills and buy her clothes since I wasn't doing it.

She knew my father was a famous surgeon and that my family had money. I guess to her that meant *I* had money. She said when she met me, she thought about giving up dancing because she really did like me but when she realized I was not going to be taking care of her, she decided to keep dancing. She never apologized. Instead, she walked away, never looking back.

I transferred to another school to avoid seeing her. It seems extreme but my heart was damaged and needed time to repair. I stayed away from the gay scene for a while. My soul was closed for renovations.

Today, Skye has her own radio show. She was quite popular in the Atlanta gay community and rumor has it her show will soon become syndicated. She speaks openly on her previous occupation on her show and at nightclubs when she is the host. I see her from time to time but hide from view. No need in rehashing that pain.

That was my only relationship with a woman but I haven't been with a man since shortly after Skye. That lasted less than a month and was just a rebound. As much as I hated the dating world in the LIFE, I couldn't seem to make myself hop back over the fence.

I came out to my parents my freshman year in college. I had a sexy, freaky roommate that walked around the dorm room naked. I had never really looked at another woman and her body fascinated me. She had the smallest waist and breasts but had a sizeable ass. The kind of ass you see on video vixens.

One night we both came in from a campus party a little high and a good bit tipsy. She stripped down as usual and got into bed. I put on my shorts and tank top and went to bed as well. I guess I had just dozed off, but I awoke to a buzzing sound followed by rustling sheets and soft moans. I recognized the buzzing as a vibrator. I had one of my own that I kept handy. But hearing hers in use was stimulating my body more than when I used mine on myself.

Her moans became louder and I could see, by the dim streetlight peeking through the window blinds, her hips rising off the bed. As my eyes got accustomed to the darkness, I could also see she had another vibrator. This one penetrating her while the other moved fervently against her clit. I didn't think it through. I just acted.

I got up from the bed, walked over to hers, kneeled beside her and took the dildo from her. She looked at me but said nothing, nor did she slow down her pelvic thrusts. I worked that dildo like I had done with my own several times. I could feel her juices dripping down the shaft which turned me on even more. I kissed her then and used my other hand to massage her small breasts.

Her moaning turned into pleas for me to fuck her. I did just that. I slammed the dildo into her waiting pussy over and over, picking up the pace when I felt hers speed up. The wet noise made my own panties damp with desire. When she came, I felt a shot of moisture all over my arm and hand. I had heard of female ejaculators but to see it for myself was surreal.

When her breathing returned to normal I simply walked back to my bed, took off my shorts, and lay down. I needed to ease the throbbing my clit was doing but I didn't think my roommate would return the favor.

As I reached under my bed for my own vibrating bullet, I felt her standing over me. She had put on a strap-on dildo and was climbing into bed with me. This was totally unexpected and I froze. She nudged my thighs apart easing herself onto the bed but instead of inserting the dildo, she buried her face in my pussy. A man before had eaten me and it was satisfactory; but what that girl did to me was unparalleled.

Her tongue licked each hole and slid up my crack, preparing my pussy for what was to come. After she fucked me with her mouth, she rose up and penetrated me with the strap. It was sizeable and hurt a bit at first but the pain eased as she stroked me to ecstasy. Never had I been fucked like that.

I knew after that night, things would never be the same for me again. My roommate and I had sex a plethora of times after that but she said she wasn't gay and although I loved every minute of it, I denied being a lesbian as well. Since that semester, I haven't seen my roommate. If I did, I would definitely have to thank her for saving me from a lifetime of mediocre sex with men.

Now, I'm single and although I'm not looking, I am hoping and praying to meet the one. Eventually. I don't want to date anymore. I just want to wake up one morning and run into her. Literally. But what's the likelihood of that happening?

CHAPTER THREE

Tori

Driving through midtown Atlanta, I am amazed at how busy the city is. Houston is considerably larger, but I think Atlanta has more people. At least it seemed that way as I sat in traffic. The thing I like about Atlanta, other than the people and the nightlife, is the landscape. There are trees everywhere. Every block has trees and some have flowers and fountains. This place is so much better to look at than Houston. And it's not nearly as hot. It's the first week in June and it's 92 degrees today. In Houston, it was 98 degrees but with the heat index it felt like 108. *Thank God I'm in Atlanta.*

The hospital is less than 10 minutes away from the condo on a non-busy weekend day. Today, the drive takes me 25 minutes. I am so glad I start my shift at six a.m. when everyone else is still in bed or just getting ready for work. I struggled to find parking but was again grateful because by this afternoon I will have assigned parking in the nearest reserved parking lot.

Atlanta General Hospital (AGH) is a large academic hospital located in the heart of midtown. It serves all ages, races, and income levels. The team of doctors that make up the university house staff and the private physicians that provide care at the facility are some of the best in the country. This is where I will work. I am an anesthesiologist and have just completed specialized training in pain management.

The Anesthesiology office is on the main level of the hospital so I stop there first to complete my paperwork. "Good morning, Dr. Becker." I was greeted by Susan, a middle-aged, white lady who is the group's secretary.

"Good morning, Mrs. Smith. How are you? It is a pleasure to see you again," I answered pleasantly. Susan was very nice to me on my initial visit to the hospital and for my interview. She even arranged my movers and the condo.

"Dr. Becker, I told you to call me Susan. I must insist," she said smiling.

"Okay Susan, but only if you call me Tori." Laughing, she agreed and showed me to my office where I completed my employment paperwork.

Once I'd printed all the documents, I turned them into her and she conducts a tour of the hospital. As we approached the operating room she tells me Dr. Smith, her husband and Chief of the anesthesia department, will continue my tour through the OR. As if on cue, the double doors open and the tall, graying, handsome white man walked towards me and gave me a big 'ole, southern hug.

"Welcome Dr. Becker. We are so glad to finally have you. How was your move?"

"It was great, Dr. Smith. Your wife made it all very convenient and painless. And please, call me Tori."

"But of course. You are one of us now. And I insist you call me William."

"Yes sir."

"No. Not sir. William."

With a smile, I replied, "Yes, William."

"Now come on. We have lots of people waiting to meet you. The female locker room is right around the corner. Here is your access key card. There should be scrubs your size in your locker. It's locker number six. I told them to make sure you got one of the larger ones. We have to treat our only female anesthesiologist well."

We shared a laugh. Susan returned to her office and I went towards the locker room.

"Tori, meet me in the physician lounge once you are done. Just follow the signs," The chief -- it's going to be hard for me to call my boss by his first name -- called over his shoulder as he headed in the direction of the male locker rooms.

I am so ecstatic about my new position and work environment that I can't stop smiling as I open the doors of the locker room and walk into the most luxurious hospital bathroom I had ever seen. Gorgeous ceramic tile covered the floor in a diagonal pattern and continue up the bottom half of the wall. Recessed can lights shone from the ceiling. The granite counter top with four deep, stainless, vanity sinks, was spacious, sparkling clean, and had two bouquets of fresh flowers one at either end of the vanity in beautiful built-in vases. There were four private showers on one wall and on further inspection I found they each had their own separate area for dressing. The main locker room area was full of cubbyholes for shoes, padded benches for changing those shoes, and stainless lockers. It was in that main space that I saw her. She was dressed in scrubs now but I would recognize that ass anywhere. In that instant, she turned towards me and smiled.

"Are you following me?" she asked.

"No, I didn't know you worked here. This really is just a coincidence," I stammered on nervously. She laughed at my obvious apprehension.

"Girl, I'm just playing with you. I see your ID badge. And trust me, I'm not scared of you. If I thought you posed a threat, I would have whooped that ass the minute you walked in here and looked through this place as if it were the Taj Mahal." She laughed again. This time I joined in.

"Hi, I'm Kenyatta, but you can call me Kenya," she said, but as she stepped closer she read my ID badge, "Oh, I am so sorry, Dr. Becker. I had no idea. We were expecting you but I didn't know you would be so young." Now she is the one babbling on nervously.

Laughing, I managed to get out, "It's okay. You can call me Tori. And as you can see, I am not old."

As she calmed down, her smile returns. "Well it is nice to finally meet you. I'm Kenya Jackson. I'm a pediatric surgery fellow but I'm doing a three month pain management rotation and I am assigned to work with you."

My stomach did several somersaults. *Am I hearing right? I have to work with this outrageously sexy girl, who happens to be my neighbor, every day for the next three months? I'm in big trouble.* I plastered on a smile and returned the formality. "It is nice to meet you as well."

"So where are you from? Where did you train? How did you pick Atlanta?"

"How do you know I'm not from Atlanta?"

"Because you don't sound like you are. And because I would have seen you at one of my rotations. You know we rotate through all the major hospitals," she stated proudly.

"You could have met me and not remembered," I teased.

Smiling she said, "No, I would have remembered that face."

And with that, I blushed like a silly little schoolgirl. Damn my fair skin. *This girl is seriously flirting with me. I am really in trouble. And how does she know I'm gay? I'm not that obvious, am I?* I was dressed comfortably but professionally and had arranged my earlier ponytail into a neat bun. Granted, my pants and shoes didn't sing femininity but I was wearing eyeliner and had even put on some eye shadow and lip-gloss in the car after she called me 'handsome' this morning. Go figure.

She grabbed her bag and said, "I'm running late but I hope to get those answers from you at a later time. It was nice meeting you and I can't wait to start working with you. I'm finishing up my pediatric critical care rotation this week and I'll be on your service as of Monday afternoon. I know there's lots you can teach me and I can't wait to learn it all." And with what I swear is a wink, she walked out the locker room leaving me with my mouth wide open.

As I sat on the bench, I said a silent prayer. *Lord, please help me not to fuck this up. This is the perfect job and I don't want to lose it over some ass.* And as an afterthought, I added, *And please forgive me for my cursing. I'm working on it.*

I found my locker and changed into scrubs. They fit perfectly. Glad that I chose to wear flat, comfortable shoes, I go to the physician lounge to meet up with the chief.

I am either going to love this place or hate it. Up until five minutes ago, I loved it. Right now, I'm not too sure.

4

CHAPTER FOUR

Kenya

OMG! I had to stop right outside the locker room to catch my breath. I couldn't believe what was happening. The hot chic from the elevator is actually my attending physician for the next three months. What had I gotten myself into? And not only is she my boss and preceptor, but I will have to work with her once I finish my training next year and for years to come.

What possessed me to flirt with her? I'm not even 'out' like that at work. And just because she wore a thumb ring and dressed like a soft stud, didn't mean she was gay. I'm 99% sure she was but that 1% could cost me a sexual harassment suit.

Yet and still, my mind couldn't help but imagine the kind of life we could have together as a couple. Two beautiful physicians doing our thing at work daily and then turning it out at home in the bedroom. Our kids would be well behaved and beautiful. *She looks like she'd make a good mommy.* We could have a large home in the suburbs and host dinner parties for our colleagues.

But the reality is, right now, she's my boss and AGH has a strict policy on fraternization between trainees and attending physicians. It is prohibited. End of story. No discussion. No debating. It is what it is and if you don't like it, find another job. That's how serious they were. In fact, one of my classmates had to transfer to another hospital because her husband took a position at AGH. She was pissed but they decided he was a better investment for the hospital.

Furthermore, I need to focus. But how on earth can I do that working with this fine woman everyday. *And*, we live next door to each other. This was going to be tough.

Walking down the hallway, I remind myself what a great opportunity I have in front of me. For all I know, Dr. Becker – Tori -- might be in a serious relationship. Rumor has it she moved here by herself but a woman as fine as she is *must* have someone. Yes, I know I'm pretty damn hot myself, but I just have bad luck when it comes to relationships. *I bet her partner is beautiful. Probably a model. Or a high-powered attorney.* I use that thought to psych myself out so I can get my game face back on.

I arrived at the pain clinic, pausing to take a deep breath before entering. The secretary/nurse greeted me with a "Good Morning. I'll be right with you," without raising her head.

My heart raced at the sound of the familiar voice. *Can this day get any more complicated?* I seriously considered walking out the office and changing my elective but that would require explanations and searching for a new preceptor and re-negotiating my employment contract since this elective was what afforded me the position. So I took a deep breath, again, and walked right up to the desk.

"Good morning, Carmen. How are you?" I asked with complete politeness.

Recognizing my voice, she looked up at me with obvious surprise. She quickly feigned calmness and rolled her eyes at me. "How may I help you Kenya? What are you doing here? You dumped me, remember?"

Wow. She was going to go there. She was really going to go there. "Carmen, I am here for work. I am doing a three-month rotation with Dr. Becker starting on Monday. I had no idea you worked here."

"A rotation for what?" she asked. I guess I never did tell her what I did for a living. We never got that far. You see, Carmen and I had a sexual association -- yes, fuck buddies -- a couple months back. It turned out that was all we could be.

"I'm doing my pediatric surgery fellowship," I said proudly, holding my chin up.

"Humph. You never mentioned you were a doctor."

"No, I didn't. It never came up."

"I see. Well, whatever. How may I help you?"

"I am supposed to meet with Dr. Sanchez to complete some paperwork. Is he here?"

"Yes." She picked up the phone and called into his office. "Dr. Sanchez, Dr. . . . ." Whispering she asked me, "What's your last name?"

"Jackson. Dr. Kenyatta Jackson" I replied.

She rolled her eyes but relayed my response. "Dr. Kenyatta Jackson is here to see you." She paused, listening for his response. "Yes sir, I'll send her right back. . . . . Yes, I will process her paperwork. Ok." She hung up.

"Dr. Sanchez asked me to secure your pain management privileges. I need your address and phone number as well as your ID badge to allow you access to the clinic after hours."

I could tell it was painful for her to have to help me. I bet she was as uncomfortable with the idea of us having to work together as I was. Feeling slightly sorry for her, I gave her the necessary information and my badge.

"Stop at the desk on your way out and I will have it here for you. His office is down the hall, the last office in the back, straight ahead."

"Thank you, Carmen."

"Whatever." And she returned to whatever she was doing when I walked in. She always did have a sassy attitude. It's a shame things didn't work out. We had amazing sex and that girl was a freak! She was still as sexy as I remember. But I sure wasn't going to be getting any love from her anytime soon. I smiled to myself remembering the fun we had.

My smile faded when the reality of the situation hit me again. My sexy ex-lover and the woman I was now crushing on will be working together. Tori looked like she would be Carmen's type. She liked those soft studs. That was one of our issues. She didn't want a woman that looked as sexy as she did. Just had to have all the attention. *But*, Tori *was* pretty damn sexy in her own way. *Wonder what she looks like in heels.* Oh well. Probably will never find out. Either way, this was going to be an interesting three months.

Tori

The tour of the operating suites went very well and I was able to meet the other partners in the group. They had a nice luncheon in my honor. It was a pleasant surprise. I was wishing I'd worn something cuter. *Oh well.*

After meeting with the other anesthesiologists, I met most of the nurses and other support staff as well as all the surgeons that were in house. Some of the nurses were hot! It's just something about a woman in scrubs that turns me on.

After the tour of the OR, the chief excused himself but told me to continue the tour on my own. I thought that was kind of rude but I plastered a smile on my face and did what the big boss told me to. The last stop was the pain clinic. It was located down the hall and around the corner from the main anesthesia office. The frosted glass entry door was being refinished with my name above the two other doctors that staffed the clinic. *Tori Becker, MD.* Tears welled in the corners of my eyes as reality of my accomplishments set in. I had come a long way. The chief must have known the effect this would have on me. I was glad he'd left me alone and grateful for the private moment.

Gathering myself, I opened the expansive door and took in my surroundings. The colorful paintings made the cream walls come to life. The office was bright and cheery. The waiting room chairs were upholstered in contemporary prints. There were tropical plants surrounding a large waterfall fountain on the wall straight ahead. Soft music was playing through the speakers. I guess there was some sort of hidden door chime because a beautiful woman emerged from one of the back offices.

"Good afternoon. Welcome to the pain clinic. Do you have an appointment?"

"No," I answered. "I'm Tori Becker. Dr. Smith told me to ask for Dr. Sanchez."

"Oh, Dr. Becker, I apologize. We were expecting you earlier."

"I'm sorry. We had lunch in the physician's lounge. It took a bit longer than expected."

"No need to apologize. Let me get Dr. Sanchez for you. And by the way, I'm Carmen. I'm the nurse coordinator for the pain clinic so we'll be working together."

The women in Atlanta are fine. Sure hope I can stay focused at work. She's probably straight anyway. Carmen is a fair-skinned woman maybe in her mid to late twenties. She is obviously biracial with naturally curly hair, hazel eyes, and small pink lips. Her petite nose had a small diamond stud in it. I noted the silver ring on her left thumb and smiled to myself. I am wearing one also and I know it is a symbol of our sexuality. She noticed me studying her ring, finally saw mine, and smiled.

"I see we have a few things in common," she said with a sly grin. "We ought to hang out some time. I can show you some places in the city. Did you move here by yourself?" I knew she was trying to find out if I was single.

"Actually, I did. All my family is back in Houston and Louisiana." I returned the grin. *She could be a good friend,* I lied to myself.

"Well before you leave the office, we should exchange numbers. There's some stuff going on this weekend that we can check out. If you're interested that is."

"Definitely. It would be nice to see what everybody keeps talking about."

She took me around to meet Dr. Sanchez, the director of the pain clinic. He is a large Puerto Rican man with huge hands and a firm grip to match.

"Dr. Becker. It is nice to finally meet you. I am so sorry I was out when you came for your interview."

"The pleasure is all mine, sir. I am looking forward to working with the man that has given this clinic such a great reputation. It is an honor to be able to work so closely with you."

I know that sounded like I was kissing major ass, but really, Dr. Sanchez is world renown for his research studies and the formation of chronic pain protocols. He is the reason I went into pain management. The nerd in me wanted so badly to sit and pick his brain but the movers were coming. Besides, I had at least the next two years to do so.

As he explained the scheduling and practice policy and procedures, my mind drifted to the two beauties I met today. Both have beautiful faces and unbelievable bodies. I knew Carmen was in the life and I think Kenya is as well but I'm not too sure. Kenya is off limits because she's my trainee so even if she was a lesbian, I'm not allowed to date her. Carmen is an employee and there are no rules against employees dating physicians. But in point of fact, I shouldn't think about dating either one because if it didn't go well, it could make things awkward in the workplace.

Even worse, there could be drama. And I don't do well with drama.

Dr. Sanchez finished up the mini-orientation and walked me back to the front desk. "You start on Monday, correct?"

"Yes sir."

"Good, because we already scheduled your first set of patients. You'll have a pediatric surgery fellow training with you for a few months. She's top of her class. Her father is head of one of the services here but I couldn't tell you which one. Dr. Martin turned in his resignation so it will be just you, me, and Dr. Jackson for a while until I can hire someone else. You came at a great time because we need your help, but it's a bad time for you because you'll pretty much be on your own right away."

"Oh, I'll be fine, sir. I used your textbook my entire fellowship so I know your protocols well."

"Great. I think you will be in the OR until noon and then your first appointment here is at 1 pm. If you feel overwhelmed, use your fellow. Kendra Jackson, I think her name is."

"Kenya Jackson, sir?" I corrected him. "Yes, I met her earlier today."

"Yes, Kenya, that's it. She is a smart young woman with a promising career ahead of her. Rumor has it she's joining the surgical staff when she completes her fellowship next year. They'd be lucky to have her. Anyway, you'll be seeing mostly surgical patients with a little chronic pain overflow here and there. Dr. Jackson came by earlier and I gave her your phone number. I hope you don't mind, but I want her to discuss her treatment plan for the Monday patients with you before she comes in. Preparation is the enemy of chaos."

"Yes sir. Thank you."

"So I'll see you on Monday."

"Yes, you have a good weekend."

"You too. And get some rest. We have a busy summer ahead of us."

Once he walked/wobbled back to his office, I went to the front desk to exchange numbers with Carmen. She was conveniently bending over in front of the file cabinet. The thin material of the scrub pants molded against her plump, firm, round . . .

"Like what you see?" she asked, not moving from her position.

I was mortified at being caught. Before I could apologize, she continued, "We had them install it about a month or two ago. The patients say the noise soothes them."

Oh, thank God! She was talking about the waterfall fountain on the big wall behind her. *Whew.*

"It's beautiful. A good choice."

She grabbed a folder from the bottom drawer then turned to hand me a piece of paper.

"Here's my number. Make sure you lock it in. I might even give you a call tonight and see how you're doing. I have your number from the personnel file." *She's flirting with me. And I think I like it.*

"Will do. Have a good evening and it was really nice meeting you Carmen."

"Trust me, the pleasure is mine. Answer when I call you later," she said with a smile.

"Yes, ma'am." I said, waving as I exited. No sooner than I made it to my car, I got a text message. "*And if you answer when I call later, the pleasure might be OURS.*"

"DAMN," I yelled as I dropped my phone. She doesn't waste any time does she? I had to shake the sexy images of what might be, out of my head. *But is* has *been a while. A little company wouldn't hurt. I better stop in at the furniture store today so she can have some nice furniture to sit on if I invite her over.*

I was cutting it close on time but I made a detour to a contemporary furniture store I'd driven by earlier that morning. They had pieces I had only seen on HGTV and in modern living magazines. Luckily for me, I had an image in mind of what I wanted my place to look like. By the time I left the store, I had purchased a low profile sectional for the living room as well as a wood and glass entertainment center, a dining set, two sets of bedroom furniture, and some decorative pieces, all to be delivered within the next four hours. I hurried home to meet the movers.

The movers were just parking the truck and my new car was already unloaded and parked in one of my assigned parking spaces. I walked around it, checking for scratches or dings. The rental car company pulled up a few minutes after I did. I completed the necessary paperwork and they drove the rental car back to the airport for me.

I showed the movers to the service elevators and began supervising the move. Since I purchased new furniture, I instructed the guys to deliver the old furniture to the nearest Goodwill. One of the men said he was just moving out of his mom's house and needed some furniture for his new place. I told him he could have it all.

The furniture delivery truck showed up just as the movers were unloading the last of my boxes. Within a few hours, all my possessions, both new and old, were moved into the loft. The mover I gave my old furniture to, convinced the others in his team to help me hang paintings and art and put the books on the bookshelves. Then they unpacked most of my boxes. Around 9 pm, the entire condo was unpacked as if I had been living there for months instead of hours.

I thanked them for their time, tipped them, then showed them to the door. I was ready to lay across my new pillowtop mattress. I showered and put on bed clothes. I was too lazy to go out and get dinner and with all that went on today, I forgot to go grocery shopping. Just as I was getting ready to call in an order for pizza, my cell rang with a number I did not recognize.

"Hello."

"Good evening, Dr. Becker. This is Kenya Jackson."

"Oh hi, Kenya. I told you to call me Tori."

"Sorry. It's habit."

"I feel you. I'm the same way."

"Well look, I didn't mean to bother you but I was wondering if we could get together, maybe Sunday evening, and go over our cases. Dr. Sanchez suggested I do so. I understand if you have plans though."

"No, no. That will be fine, Kenya. We can . . ." I paused as I heard a beep indicating I have another call. "Can you hold on just one minute? I have a call coming in."

"No, you go ahead. I'll give you a call on Sunday to confirm."

"Ok. You have a good night."

"You too, Dr. Becker."

"Kenya, call me Tori."

Laughing she said, "Oh yea, I'm sorry. Bye."

"Bye." I clicked over, "Hello."

"Hi Tori. It's me, Carmen. Did I catch you at a bad time?"

"No, I was just about to order pizza."

"Well don't do that. I am on my way over with dinner. Do you like Indian food? I know a great spot in midtown."

"I've only had it one time but I did like it when I tried it. But really, I can just order a pizza. You don't even know where I live. What if I live 45 minutes away?" I teased.

"Then I would just have to bring an overnight bag," she quipped back. I liked her assertiveness. "Besides, I do know where you live. I went with Susan to secure the loft for you. I'll be there in 30 minutes. And I'll have my overnight bag." And with that, she hung up, leaving me with my jaw hanging in disbelief.

This girl wasted no time. I needed to get a handle on things before they got out of control. *Is this really about to happen? I hope I can slow her down if it came to that.* I should have called her back to cancel, but a part of me did want her company. I needed to talk to someone.

I called the only person who would truly understand my dilemma. My homegirl, Lisa, back in Houston. Lisa and I fooled around for a hot minute but it never went any further than that. She was still in love with her ex-girlfriend, and I was too busy with medical school to commit to anything serious. We had great sex but decided friends with benefits was the most we could be. She ended up getting back with her ex and we remained friends. We've been tighter than Speedos on a fat man ever since. She's seen all the drama I've had with women and gives me straightforward advice. She was blunt but honest.

She answered on the first ring. "Dimwit!" That was her pet name for me. "I was wondering when the hell you were gonna call me."

"Lis! How you doing Bighead?"

"Yo momma's daughter got a big head. Where the hell you been, Tori?"

"Girl, I was so busy today. I had to go by the hospital to finish paperwork and get a tour of the place again. They threw me a nice little luncheon. I have a private office with all the comforts. Leather chair, huge desk, and sweet computer. You should see the place."

"Oh trust, I will. I'm coming for your birthday. Remember? I expect a tour missy."

"I can do that. So check, I need your opinion on something."

I imagined her rolling her eyes. "Oh Lord, chile. You met a woman already?"

"Girl, no. I met two!"

"Damn, Tori! You saving any for me?"

"Now you know your ass won't look to another woman but Toya. Anyway, so, one of the girls lives in my building. On my floor."

She interrupted, "Oh hell no! That's too damn close for comfort. Next."

Laughing I said, "Let me finish. So I see this fine chic on the elevator and she has the same car as mine."

"The Benz? Damn, she rolling like that?"

"You know, I actually don't know. She couldn't be making that much. She's a fellow at the hospital."

She interrupted again in a loud voice, "Wait a damn minute! At your hospital?"

"I don't own the hospital Lisa, but yeah."

"Heffa, you know what I meant. Wow, that really is too close, Tori."

"But wait, it gets better. She's a pediatric surgery fellow doing a pain management rotation. And guess who's going to be training her for the next three months?"

"Tori Becker! Tell me you are fucking kidding me."

"Nope, dead serious."

"Wow."

"But check this, Lis. This chic is so fine. She was in the elevator in some running shorts showing off her perfect legs and thighs and oh my gosh, the ass! Had my mouth watering. She has this slim waist and flat stomach. And her breasts were so damn nice. You know I'm not big on boobies unless they're small and perky. Hers were probably a B, maybe C cup, but *damn* they looked good."

"Girl, leave it alone. I don't care how fine she is. And how did she manage to buy a car like that, anyway? You don't know what that chic is up to on the side. You know, they say all the women that work in the strip clubs in Atlanta are either in law school or med school."

"Nah, I can't even see her doing that."

"Tori, you still don't get it. Leave that girl alone. Tell me about the next one."

Sighing, I gave up on telling her about Kenya. "Okay, so the next chic, her name is Carmen. She's mixed. A cute little thing. Real petite. Maybe 5'2. Tight body. Hazel eyes. Cute, curly 'fro. The girl has booty for days."

"And we *know* you like your ass." We both laughed. "Where'd you meet her?"

I didn't want to answer her.

"Tori. I know you heard me. Where'd you meet her?"

I still didn't answer. I didn't want her to pop my bubble again.

"Tori Lashae Becker!"

"Damn, Lisa. You don't have to call me by my whole government name."

"Well answer my question. Does she live in your building too? What? The whole damn building is gay?"

I couldn't answer for about 30 seconds because I was too busy cracking up. That's why I love Lisa. The girl speaks her mind. No matter how crazy it sounded to the average ear.

"No, Lisa. She's the nurse in the pain clinic."

"Humph. So will you get in trouble if you date her?"

"No."

"But if things don't work out, you could have drama at your job."

"Yes."

"I dunno, T. Maybe you should wait a while before you ask her out. See how crazy she is."

"Ummmmm ... "

"You asked her out already, didn't you?" Again, I could see her rolling her eyes *and* having her hands on her hips.

"Not exactly. She kinda invited herself over for dinner. In fact, she's on her way here right now. And she said she's bringing an overnight bag."

"Whoaaaa! Wait one damn minute! You've been in Atlanta not even 24 hours yet, and already you getting pussy thrown at you? Shit, I need to take my ass back to medical school." This time, we both laughed uncontrollably. The ringing house phone interjected.

"Hold on Lisa." I ran to answer it. "Hello."

"It's Carmen. I'm at the gate."

"Ok, park in spot 43. Then you have to buzz again to enter the elevator lobby."

I pushed the button allowing her to enter the parking garage. Going back to the phone I said, "Lisa, I gotta go."

"She sounds hella sexy but be careful my friend. Call me first thing when she leaves in the morning. I want to hear all about this."

"You know I don't kiss and tell."

"Since when, heffa?"

"Whatever. I'll call you tomorrow."

"Have fun, be safe."

"Alright, bye." I hung up quickly and ran to answer the second buzzer to let her into the lobby. I liked the extra security in this building.

Running to my room, I exchanged my shorts and wife beater for a tank top and some jeans. By the time I was buttoning the pants, the doorbell was ringing. I was so nervous but I collected my courage and opened the door.

5

CHAPTER FIVE

Tori

Carmen was sexy when I saw her earlier today, but standing at my door, the girl was drop dead gorgeous. She was wearing a cream sleeveless shirt with a plunging neckline, tan colored khaki short shorts that molded every curve of her hips and ass, and brown high-heeled sandals. Her hair was still in the curly style but she had a large flower with shades of brown, clipped in on one side. Where her face was free of makeup earlier, tonight she was wearing eyeliner, eye shadow, and lip-gloss, in neutral colors. And she smelled so good.

I must have been just standing there staring at her because she laughed at me and said, "You gonna take one of these bags and let me in?"

I was so embarrassed. Blushing, I replied, "Sorry, come on in." I took the bags from her and allowed her to enter. "You look great."

She turned again to face me. With my bare feet and her in heels, we were almost eye-to-eye. She stepped forward and kissed my lips ever so lightly. Nothing more than a peck, but I felt a jolt of electricity going from my lips, down to my stomach, and ending at that spot between my thighs.

"You look pretty good yourself."

I took the bags in the kitchen, still tingling from her teasing kiss. She came into the kitchen behind me, slowly looking around. "I love what you've done with the place. The furniture fits perfectly. And you have some nice art pieces in the living room."

"Thanks. I stopped at the furniture store today and had them deliver most of this stuff," I said, gesturing to the living and dining room furniture.

"Well you did an amazing job in a short time. I should have you help me pick out some pieces for my townhouse. I moved in a couple months ago and still haven't been able to commit to any furniture for the formal rooms."

"Sure, that sounds like fun. Whenever you're ready. So what do we have to eat?" I asked, peeking into the bags. She slapped at my hands.

"Nuh unh. No, ma'am. First, you give me a tour of your bachelor pad." She grabbed my hand and pulled me out of the kitchen.

"You are pretty aggressive. You know that?"

"Is that a problem?"

"No. It's kinda cute." Noticing her blush, I teased her further. "You know you're turning red, right?"

"Oh hush," she said with a bashful smile. "So you think I'm cute?"

I'm not sure where the sudden rush of boldness came from, but I took the extra step and went right up to her, looked her dead in the eyes, and said, "No, I don't think you're cute. I think you're hot. Sexy. Gorgeous. Fine. Beautiful. None of those words are an adequate description."

She was speechless. So I took advantage of the moment and leaned in to kiss her. Her lips were so soft. And after a couple seconds, she surprised *me* by slipping her tongue between my lips. She took time to taste them before deepening the kiss. My hands slid around to caress her back and pull her into me. Her soft curves melted against mine. Her hands did some exploration of their own and found their way under the bottom edge of my tank. They lingered there, her fingers playing across my stomach. When I felt her hands climbing further up, I broke the kiss, not ready for how fast things were going. I stepped back and dropped my hands. Her eyes opened and smiled at me.

"Nice. Hope I didn't scare you, doc."

Grinning like a Cheshire cat, I replied, "Not even. I just don't want to rush things. We still have to work together."

Sighing and raising her hands in surrender, she said, "I knew you would say that. And I guess you're right. But when you came into that office today, I said to myself, 'Now that's my type!' You had that 'tweener' look going on and I thought it was so hot!"

Clueless, I asked, "Umm, what's a tweener?"

"A tweener is a lesbian that looks androgynous enough that you can't tell if she's a femme or a stud. Nobody's ever called you that?"

"No. And I don't think I'm a tweener. I mean, I wear some not so feminine clothes at times but I will switch up and wear some fitted pants and heels in a minute. I think I'm just flexible."

"Well, that's the other definition of a tweener. A lesbian that is 'unlabeled' or that can bounce back and forth *between* the two looks. Hence the title, 'tweener'."

"Oh. I guess when you put it like that. So you like tweeners huh? Is that the only type of woman you date? And do you date guys too?"

She rolled her eyes at me.

I asked, "What was that for?"

"No, I am not bi. That's an insult."

"Why you say that?"

"Because bisexual women are trifling hoes."

Surprised by her bluntness, I responded, "That's not always true. Some bisexual women are just 'tweeners'. They are comfortable with either sex, just like a tweener is comfortable with either look. It doesn't mean they are dating men and women at the same time. It just gives them more options."

"Tori, are you telling me you're bisexual?"

Laughing, "Girl, no. But I respect their desire to be more open-minded. Would I date one? No. But that's just my preference."

"Oh ok. Just making sure."

"So answer my question. Do you only date tweeners?"

"No, I date whoever I feel like dating. I don't usually date hard studs though. You?"

"I usually date feminine women. I've dated studs before but I'm not submissive enough for them."

We returned to the kitchen to eat dinner. The Indian food was great. It had a nice, spicy kick to it. Curry chicken and curry goat, some rice, and some sort of flat bread looking thing. It was very delicious. We had a few glasses of Moscato with the meal. By the time we were finished eating, we had exchanged background information, talked about our history and our future, our likes and dislikes.

I learned Carmen was the product of a Jamaican mother and a white American father. They met when her father was on his honeymoon with his wife in Jamaica. Her father fell in love with her mother and never returned to the United States. His wife was, of course devastated, and every few months, even to this day, still sends hate mail to her parents. They married after the other marriage was annulled. She has three siblings but she is the only one in the states. The others are in England and Jamaica. Her family knows she is gay and accepts it, although they were heartbroken at first.

She moved to the states once she finished high school and worked while attending nursing school. She worked as an ICU nurse before accepting a position as a pain nurse. After proving her capabilities, she was promoted to coordinator. She was hoping to complete her Master's degree in Nursing in August and will be taking a position with another anesthesia company.

"See. So we won't be working together for long. This doesn't have to be awkward," she said, trying to convince me.

I thought about it and what she said made sense. We would have two more months of working together. Surely things couldn't get bad in that short a time.

"You make a good point."

"So can we continue where we left off," she asked slyly as she walked over to where I am sitting and straddled me so were face to face. We kissed deeply, tasting the wine on each other's tongue. Her hands released my hair from the loose ponytail and massaged my scalp. This reminded me of that portion of my dream from earlier that morning. Her ass made slow circles across my pelvis. She kissed my neck as I released the clip from her hair and slowly slid her shirt up and over her head.

Her small breasts were bare in front of me. Cream colored with a pinkish-tan nipple. The breasts were just a little more than a mouthful. Just the way I like them. My hands caressed her breasts and unable to hold back, I took the left one in my mouth, using my tongue to flick against her nipple. She threw her head back and moaned. Her hips circled with more zeal, encouraging me to continue with the task at hand. Needing to be fair, I turned my attention to her right breast and gave the same treatment.

Pausing only to pull my tank top over my head to release my own breasts, my tongue continued to taste her creamy flesh. I suggested we take it to the bedroom. We undressed in the dim light of the bedside lamps and lay on the king size bed. Our legs became entwined as we squirmed against each other. I wanted to take it slow, since it was our first time, but the fire inside wouldn't allow it.

I guided her to climb on top of me and had her position her hips above my face. Her freshly shaven pussy was right in front of my face and the heat from it called to me. With one long lick from her slit to her clit, she shivered above me. I repeated with short strokes, then long ones, followed by little swirls. Her body rewarded me by leaking some of it's sweet juices.

Her wetness covered my chin and lips, which made me want even more. My tongue dove in and penetrated her like a dick. I plunged in and out, stopping to add a little sucking to her clit. She grabbed hold of the headboard and rode my face like a cowgirl. Even though her new position decreased my oxygen supply, my hands cupped her round ass and helped her gyrate more efficiently. I pulled my head away to gasp for air before returning to the task at hand.

One of her hands reached back to help her stabilize herself as her other hand found its way between my thighs to stimulate my hot box. I could feel my moistness on her fingers as her thumb rubbed my clit and two fingers slipped into my pussy. Her exploits brought me closer and closer to climax as her moans grew louder and hips moved faster against my face. I stopped licking and probing with my tongue and concentrated on her clit. I alternated sucking and licking that little button until it grew to twice its original size.

Sounds of our lovemaking filled the air. Her moans and freaky babble drowned out the sound of the music being played on the MP3 player in the living room. "Fuck me!" she yelled. I managed to use three fingers on one hand to penetrate her and massage her inside walls while using my mouth to apply suction to her clit. At the same time she withdrew her fingers from me and used her thumb and index finger to knead my clit.

The lubrication and friction was enough to take me over the edge just as she jerked from her own climax. Her sweet juices dripped down my chin, leaving a trail on my neck and chest. She circled her hips a few more times for good measure before collapsing on me. Taking a moment to catch our breaths, we gazed at each other. We kissed deeply, me letting her taste herself. She smiled intently.

"Oh my gosh! Girl, you just shocked the hell outta me. Didn't know you could take charge like that." We laughed at that.

"Whatever. Guess I'll have to show you."

"I guess so." We kissed and she snuggled against me. "I'm calling out tomorrow. Do you have plans?"

"No, was just going to go grocery shopping."

"Ok cool. I can take you to the farmer's market. You can get all types of meats and fruits and vegetables. There's even a little eatery inside."

"Hey, thanks. I don't know my way around yet so I appreciate the help."

"Anything for you."

We talked until the sun started peeking through the windows. It was then that we fell asleep.

6

CHAPTER SIX

Kenya

Ok. So I was a little jealous when I saw Carmen stepping off the elevator. I knew she wasn't coming to see me and there was only one other person she would be visiting. Tori. *That bitch moves fast.* Now I was wishing I *did* invite Tori out tonight.

I was heading out that Thursday night. After meeting Tori earlier that day and then running into Carmen in the pain clinic, I really needed to get out and get a drink. I thought of inviting Tori to come with me but I still hadn't decided if I was willing to cross that line. And was she even single?

When I called to let her know we ought to discuss our cases, I was going to ask her out, but I chickened out when she received another call. I took it as a sign that I should keep it strictly professional.

As soon as I hung up the phone from her, it rang. Looking at the caller ID, I saw it was Jewelle, a realtor I met at a Memorial Day weekend party. Jewelle was in her early thirties but dominated the Atlanta real estate market. She was classic southern beauty with medium brown skin, jaw length bob with bronze highlights, perky breasts, small waist, thick thighs, and hellacious ass. I had seen her billboard ads across the city but never imagined she would be gay. When I met her that night, we exchanged numbers but this was the first time she was calling me.

"Hello," I answered the phone after a couple rings.

"Hi. Is this Kenya?" she inquired.

"Yes, it is. May I ask who's calling?"

"Hi girl. This is Jewelle Armstrong. I met you at the Women That Play party last month. How are you?"

"I'm well. I didn't expect to hear from you," I said honestly.

"I had all intentions of calling you honey but things have been so busy. I actually had an appointment with your father today. I've known Dr. Jackson for years and it never occurred to me that you were his daughter. I actually closed the deal on your condo last year."

"Oh wow. What a coincidence!" Such a small world.

"That's what *I* thought. Anyway, he said you might be looking for a house to be built within the next year or so and he wanted me to help you."

This was news to me. Sure, I had mentioned to my parents that I really wanted a house in the suburbs but my father was so adamant about me staying closer to the hospital.

"Well, I *am* interested but I haven't even started looking at areas or what builders I would consider."

"And that's where I come in. Why don't we meet up for drinks and chitchat? I'd love to hear your wish list. I'm hosting a little get together at a warehouse near downtown. I can text you the address."

"That actually sounds pretty good. I'm off tomorrow anyway. How should I dress?"

"Classy but sexy. It's a special party. I think you'll like it. It starts at 11:00 pm. I'll text you the password as well. See you in a bit."

"Ok, thanks." I wondered what type of party this was. Maybe some sort of secret association. I had heard of an organization in town with nothing but professional lesbians. The primary requirement was an individual salary of at least $100,000. I didn't make that much. Not yet, anyway. Maybe she knew I was finishing up my training soon.

Thinking this must be an invitational, I pulled out a sexy black dress that revealed just enough cleavage and fit nicely to my hips and ass, but was still sophisticated. Black Manolo Blahniks and matching clutch purse, diamond earrings, and a silver necklace with simple diamond pendant completed the outfit. I curled my hair, put on makeup, and a dab of body oil.

I made it to the elevator but the door opened before I pushed the button. Carmen stepped off. She looked at me appreciatively before speaking. "Looking good, Kenya."

"Thank you." She was looking pretty damn good too. But I knew why she was there.

"Night on the prowl? I mean town." She laughed menacingly.

"Carmen, you're one to talk. Here to see Tori huh?"

She stepped to me making me step backward into the elevator. She came into the elevator and pushed the button for the ground floor. When it started to descend, she pushed the STOP button.

"What the hell are you doing?" I yelled at her.

"Just trying to talk to you. Tori and I are a couple. I don't want you around her except when you are at the hospital. Don't tell her we slept together. I'm not asking you. I'm telling you. If you fuck this up for me, I will be sure everyone at the hospital knows all about your lifestyle."

I couldn't believe this little bitch was threatening me. I was so angry I could have choked her but in my calmest voice I replied, "You are pitiful. If I wanted Tori, you wouldn't be paying her a visit right now. You are nothing but a greedy slut looking for your meal ticket. I don't give a damn about you or whatever relationship you might have. Stay out of my way and I'll stay out of yours."

"Humph. Can't say I didn't warn you."

I reached around her and pushed the RUN button. I didn't have time to play games with this little girl. I was very close to hitting her and I didn't need *that* messing up my career. As I was exiting the elevator I said smugly over my shoulder, "Tell Tori I'll see her on Sunday."

"Bitch!" She yelled as the doors closed.

With the adrenaline rush from the confrontation, I sped to the address I received by text message. The location was near Georgia Tech downtown. The parking lot surrounding the warehouse was nearly full with luxury cars and SUVs.

The door was manned by an off duty female police officer I had seen at the club a few times and a tall Hispanic woman who looked like a Victoria's Secret model. She didn't smile at me until I gave her the password. She escorted me into the building as another model-type woman took her spot at the door. Just inside, I saw several more model-looking women waiting their turn to escort the guests inside.

Passing through the entrance hallway, we entered into a large open room with a well stocked bar at one end, a stage and DJ booth at the other, and restaurant style booths along one side. The open area seemed to be a dance floor and sexy women dancing to Usher's 'Lil Freak' already occupied it. There were so many sexy women and a few more 'models' all over the room.

I made my way to the bar and noticed my escort still at my side. I turned to tell her thank you but she placed her hand in the small of my back and accompanied me to the bar. There, I told her "Thank you."

She simply smiled and said, "You're welcome. My name is Maria and I'll be your servant for the rest of the night. Anything you need, anything at all, just let me know. This is an open bar. You tell me what you want and I will tell the bartender. I am not allowed to get drinks for you due to safety concerns but once you get your drink, I can show you to your room and . . ."

I was looking at her as if she were crazy. I had no idea what she was talking about. She seemed to realize this and asked, "She didn't tell you did she?"

"No. What type of party is this?"

"Ms. Armstrong throws one of these parties every month for singles only. They are by invitation only. Every month, there are four to five new members. You are one of them. Since we lose members to relationships every month, we try to keep a steady influx of new members. Each member gets a private room upstairs. You can use the room any way you choose. They are soundproofed. Each member also has a servant assigned. The servants are at your disposal for dancing, conversation, massages, private shows. Even sex is allowed. The only rules are you have to get your own drinks from the bar, no cameras are allowed, and you are sworn to secrecy You can invite another guest next month but it would have to be approved through Ms. Armstrong."

While she was explaining, I was taking in my surroundings. I saw what must be the world's largest bed rise up out of the middle of the dance floor. She giggled and said, "And that's where the magic happens. That's the party platform. It's pretty much a free for all."

I was nervous. I had heard of parties like this for couples and some for singles but never did I think I would attend one of them. She seemed to sense my fear. "Don't be scared. You don't have to participate if you don't want to."

I smiled at her. She was very nice. I told her I needed a drink to help calm my nerves. A dirty martini. She ordered one for the both of us and then we made our way upstairs to the private rooms. There was a long hall with doors on either side. Each door was numbered. I finished my drink before we even made it to the door. The room was set up like a hotel suite with a large king size bed with nightstands, a flat screen TV, DVD player and stereo system in a small media console, and a wet bar with mini-refrigerator. There was a bathroom with shower and tub combination. It was all very clean and lavishly decorated.

There was a knock at the door. Maria opened it and Jewelle walked in. "Kenya, good to see you again," she said as she walked over and gave me a hug and kiss on the cheek. "How do you like it so far?"

She was stunning. She wore a turquoise mini dress that accentuated her curves. Her hair was loosely flowing around her face and with just a hint of make-up, she was absolutely beautiful.

"Girl, I wish you would have told me what this was," I whispered.

"If I had told you, would you have come?"

"Probably not. This is a little out there for me."

"I know. That's why I didn't tell you. But once you experience it tonight, you won't hesitate to come back. It's a great gathering place for professional, single lesbians whether you are looking for a relationship or just sex. And it's the best of the best here. The crème de la crème. I made sure you got Maria. She's one of the best. Use her wisely." She winked at me.

"Maria has been very good to me. But I don't think I can *use* her."

"Sure you can. In fact, I'd like to see you *use* her." She beckoned to Maria and dimmed the lights. My heart began racing as Maria dropped the straps of her dress from her shoulders and stepped out of her black dress. Her hair fell against her bare back as she removed the clip that was holding it in place. She was naked with nothing on but her stilettos. I turned to Jewelle and she was also stepping out of her dress while looking at me and smiling.

"Ummm, Jewelle, I don't think I can do this," I said uneasily.

"Well don't do anything," she said as she kicked off her shoes and the dress. She stood in front of me with her perfect breasts and slim waist. I could see her belly button ring, a small tattoo that circled her waist like a belt, and a clit ring was peeking out at me from that place between her thighs.

Maria came to stand behind me and began kissing my neck. I closed my eyes in anticipation. Her warm lips left a trail of kisses down my neck and nibbled on each ear. She reached around and caressed my breasts through the thin fabric of my dress. A moan escaped my lips.

Jewelle's hands reached around and palmed my ass, giving it a gentle squeeze. She kissed me on the lips, softly as first but then hungrily. Her tongue pushed its way into my mouth. My tongue danced with hers and I succumbed to the moment. My hands that had been stiff against my sides reached and pulled Jewelle closer, molding her body against mine.

I felt as Maria unzipped my dress and it fell to the floor. She kissed her way down my back, pausing at my butt cheeks and nibbling on each one. She continued down each of my legs and kissed her way back up. She blew a warm breath on that spot that was now moist and hot. A shiver ran down my spine.

Maria helped me out of my dress and thongs then sat me on the bed while Jewelle watched. She kneeled in front of me and kissed my breasts. She buried her head in between my legs and suckled on my clit. She ate my pussy as if she was starving. My eyes closed tight as I enjoyed the moment. I moaned, I squealed, and I pushed her head deeper, encouraging her to fuck me with her tongue. It penetrated me as I felt the bed give under new weight.

Jewelle pushed me back onto the bed and positioned herself above my face. She lowered herself to my waiting tongue and I tasted her. Not too sweet but definitely a hint of sweetness. My tongue flicked against her clit ring and she moaned in pleasure.

I was in heaven as Maria stroked me with her tongue and fingers and Jewelle rode my face. I came in no time and Maria pushed my thighs up to my chest where they rested against Jewelle's back. She straddled my crotch and I felt her wetness blend with mine as she rode my pussy. Our clits kissed on their own accord. Her hands played with Jewelle's breasts as she rode me. Her seductive moans filled the room as she rocked back and forth. Her clit was long and fucked me like a small penis, dipping in and out of my pussy.

Jewelle turned around to face her and they kissed eagerly. Maria never broke stride as she rode me again to ecstasy. Jewelle came shortly after and then Maria's high-pitched moans let me know she too was climaxing.

The three of us lay for a few minutes caressing each other and catching our breaths. Jewelle got up and freshened up in the bathroom saying she had to make sure things were going well downstairs. She closed the door behind her and left the suite.

Meanwhile, Maria went to the nightstand and produced a large black strap on, probably about 10 inches. I looked at her like she was crazy. I was not going to let a stranger penetrate me like that. She clarified, "I want you to use this on me." I took it from her as she handed it to me. I had never used one before but had wanted to ever since Carmen had told me she liked being fucked with one.

She helped me strap it on and pulled me on top of her to lie in the bed. She guided the tip to her entrance and I slowly inched it in, trying not to hurt her. She moaned and gripped at my hips, slamming the dildo into her waiting pussy. This was enough to drive me wild. I thrusted into her over and over again, each time going deeper. I grabbed her thighs and pushed them to her chest as she had done to me. She grabbed her ankles and extended them to the headboard. She raised her hips to meet each of my thrusts. I was feeling so good but not wanting to cum again.

After a few minutes of this, I helped her onto her knees and she held on to the headboard. I stroked her doggie style watching her ass bounce. I tweaked and pulled at her nipples. I kissed her neck. I pulled at her hair. I was losing control. She flipped me over and straddled me, re-inserting the dildo herself. She rocked her hips, gyrated her pelvis, and rode my temporary dick as if her life depended on it. Her breasts bounced up and down and her hair stuck to her face as she did her thing. She came with a loud moan, collapsing on top of me and kissed me passionately. She helped me remove the strap, then we had mutual pleasure in the 69 position.

Even after that, I still wanted more. We got in the shower together and pleasured each other there as well. By the time we got done, it was almost 3 am and the party was winding down. We joined the others downstairs and I was excited to see Jewelle 'entertaining' her guests on the platform. She was wearing a large strap-on and had a blonde girl kneeling in front of her, sucking it. I smiled at her and she winked at me before turning back to the girl. I made my way to the door.

Maria walked me to my car and we exchanged numbers. She told me that tonight was her last night at the club because she was graduating from law school the following weekend. She wanted to spend more time with me. Get to know me. I gave her my number but told her I wasn't looking for anything serious. She kissed me as I sat in the driver's seat, slipping her hand under my thongs to stroke my clit. Right there in the driver's seat of my open car, she stroked me to seventh heaven. She said, "We'll see about that." Then she closed my door, walked away, and I drove home, sated.

7

CHAPTER SEVEN

Tori

The next morning, Carmen and I slept in until shortly before noon. Of course, we had sex a few more times. It was like we couldn't get enough of each other. Even throughout the day as we grocery shopped, drove around town, and made dinner, we held hands, kissed, and even had sex in the car at the park. I was enjoying myself and she seemed to be doing the same. She spent that night and the next with me as well.

On Sunday, after I dropped several hints, she invited me to see her house. Carmen lived in Decatur, near Lithonia, a suburb east of Atlanta. She lived in a new, three-story townhouse in a quiet, gated community. On the lower level was a garage and finished basement with game room, media room, and exercise room. The next level had a large family room, with attached kitchen and breakfast area, as well as a formal dining room and guest bedroom. The master bedroom, master bath, and third bedroom were on the upper level. There was also a separate loft area, which she was currently using as office space.

"Girl, this house is huge! What do you need all this space for?"

"It's not *that* big. Besides, I would like to have kids and a family one day."

"Yeah, but right now, it's just you."

"Well not really, my ex-husband lives here too."

This shocked the hell out of me. In all the many hours of conversation we'd had, not once had she mentioned a husband. "Carmen, what husband?"

"He's my *ex*-husband. And we only got married so I could get my citizenship papers."

"Okay, so why didn't you tell me? And if he's your ex-husband, why does he still live here?"

I could see her getting angry but so was I. I felt she had been dishonest by leaving that important piece of information out.

"First off, he's my ex. We bought this house together so until we can figure out what to do with it, we're stuck here together. Second, I didn't think it was important. Like I said, he's my *ex!* I'm telling you about it now. You can either trust me or don't." By that time, her tone had changed and her volume increased significantly. "If I was hiding something, why would I have invited you here?"

"You know what? I don't know. I'm going to head home, I have to get ready for work tomorrow." I turned around to leave but she grabbed my arm.

"Tori. Look, I'm sorry. I wanted to tell you but I wasn't sure how you would react. Like I said, the only reason we got married was so I could get my papers. Now that I have them, we are getting a divorce."

Realizing what she just said, I lost my cool. Now it was my turn to yell. "You just finished telling me he's your ex-husband. And now you say you are *about* to get a divorce. Which one is it because I am hella confused right now?"

"He's my ex-husband because what we had is over."

"But you said it was *just* for your papers."

"Yes, the marriage was for our papers but we did love each other at one point . . ."

I didn't stick around to hear anything else. As far as I was concerned, I had heard all I needed to hear. As I was pulling out the driveway, Carmen ran to the driver's door.

With tears running down her cheeks, she said, "Tori, I'm sorry. I'm not lying to you. I just didn't want *this* to happen."

Unable to hold my tongue, I replied, "So what you are telling me is that you are no better than the bisexual women you were so turned off by the other night." I never heard her response. I sped out of her subdivision and headed back to the loft. That was the shortest relationship I had ever had.

I made it back to the parking garage just as Kenya was unloading shopping bags from her car. I didn't want to be rude but I wasn't in the mood for conversing either. I opted for middle ground. "Good afternoon, Dr. Jackson," I said politely.

With her flirty smile she replied, "I thought we were on first name basis by now Dr. Becker."

I couldn't help but smile.

She continued, "And how are you? You're not looking too happy. Long weekend?" She smiled as if she knew about my weekend rendezvous. Before I could answer she confirmed. "I saw you and Carmen as you were getting on the elevator earlier. Don't worry. You're secret's safe with me."

Ok, so I was worried. Not so much about being outed at the job. I didn't try to hide that. But ever since my last few run-ins with coworkers, I've tried to keep my love life away from the workplace. And usually, I never had reason for concern because the women had as much on the line as I did.

My thoughts must have been written all over my face. In a serious tone, she said, "Seriously, I'm not going to tell anybody. I just want you to be careful. That girl is something else. I know you're feeling her and all but there's a lot you can't see. It's not my place to tell you but I don't want my mentor to be in a funky mood and mess up my rotation because of women and their drama."

I could see her point. It was obvious that after just one weekend, I had already had a date with drama. And with the way I was feeling, I'm sure it would carry over to the following week. Especially having to work with Carmen for the next two months. And to think, just two days ago I told myself nothing could go that bad in two months. If I weren't so upset, I would find it funny.

"Kenya, you have nothing to worry about. I know how to remain professional."

"Ok, Dr. Becker. I was just saying . . ."

"I understand your concern. I am telling you; you have nothing to worry about. And again, call me Tori."

"So, we're back to first names now?" Laughing, she said, "Good. Now help me with these bags, *Tori.*" I couldn't help but join in her laughter.

"Did you buy up the whole mall?" I teased.

"Ha-ha, very funny. No, had to pay a visit to Atlantic Station. H&M had a sale and Victoria's secret is having their Semi-Annual Sale. You should check it out."

"I love H&M. We don't have one in Houston."

"I love them too. Besides, I needed some new things for next weekend. Are you and Carmen going to any of the events?"

"What events?

"National gay pride weekend. They are having all these parties and picnics. You should check them out. I'm surprised she hasn't mentioned them to you. She promotes with one of the groups that host the parties."

I heard every word she said but my mind was focusing on what it all meant. So Miss Kenya was in the life. Interesting. "Interesting."

"What? You've never heard of Pride?" she asked oblivious to her confession.

"No, I've heard of it. Just didn't think you would want to go. I thought it was for the LGBT population." I couldn't help but laugh.

"I guess you think you've busted me, but like I said, your secret's safe with me. I hope you can say the same of mine."

"I got you. No worries. Now can you use your free hand and push the button for our floor." We'd been standing in the unmoving elevator for at least a minute before I realized neither of us had pushed the button.

"Oh, my bad." Laughter filled the elevator. "And don't think I didn't notice you went and got a car like mine. Cute. I like your rims better than mine."

"That was a graduation/birthday gift from my parents and the rims were something they threw in to seal the deal."

"Wow. My dad bought mine a couple months ago when I told him I was taking the position at AGH after fellowship. He did his residency and fellowship there as well. When's your birthday?"

"Really? Your dad's a surgeon?"

"Yeah. Neurosurgery. He was disappointed that I didn't follow all the way in his footsteps. He says general pediatric surgeons don't make as much as neurosurgeons but it wasn't about the money for me. I mean, yes, it held some weight, but not as much as just doing what I love. I love kids. And don't think I didn't notice you ignored my question. When was your birthday?"

Smiling, I answered, "Next Saturday."

Even as the elevator door opened, I stood there impressed. This girl was super sexy, obviously smart, and now it seems, has a heart and strong will. I let her off the elevator first. Today she was wearing a strapless top, skinny jeans with stilettos, and her hair was down in a layered style that came a few inches below her shoulders. It looked freshly done. "Your hair looks nice."

She stopped and turned around. "Is that the only thing that looks nice?" She was flirting with me. Teasing me really. She laughed before I could respond. "Just kidding. I know Carmen already marked her territory. So will you come out next weekend for the festivities and to celebrate your birthday?"

I simply smiled and shrugged. I didn't have any plans but I didn't want to be around Carmen and Kenya at the same time either. It was going to be hard enough managing the temptation at work.

We were at the door of her condo and I was glad for the distraction as she fumbled with the bags to unlock the door. When she finally managed to open the door, she invited me in. "Come on in, I make a mean margarita. Put the bags over there on the couch."

Her condo layout was a mirror image of mine. She too, had contemporary furniture but her walls were painted and she had many more pieces of artwork. From where I stood, I could see that she used her spare bedroom as an office/home gym. She seemed to have a better view of the city as well.

She noticed my examination and said "My dad bought the condo when they first started building them. The builder is an old friend of his. He bought the penthouse as well and wanted me to live there once I finish this fellowship but I told him I want to live in the suburbs and start my family. Right now they are using it for corporate leases."

That was the second time for the day I had heard about plans for a family and I really wasn't in the mood for it. "I'll let you get settled. I have to do some things to get ready for the first day at the new job so just call me when you're ready to discuss the cases."

My sudden change of mood caught her off guard. "Did I say something to offend you?"

"No. Why would you say that?"

"Because you are bolting out of here as if I did."

"Well, no. You didn't."

"Good. So stay and have a margarita with me. I'll even share some of my mom's cooking with you. Every Sunday she cooks an enormous meal and makes me bring a ton of it home because she has nowhere to store it all and nobody to eat it. This week it's fried chicken, but it's spicy."

"My folks are from Louisiana. I can handle spicy." The mood had become light again with the talk of food. What can I say? I love to eat.

"Then you'll like this. She's from Louisiana too. She also made macaroni and cheese, greens, cornbread, sweet potato pie, and for dessert, peach cobbler."

"Wow, my mouth's watering, for real."

"Well sit down, let me throw on some comfy clothes and get started with the margaritas."

She went into the master bedroom and pulled the door closed slightly. I could hear her moving around, opening and closing doors. In the meanwhile, my phone rang. It's Carmen. "Hello."

"Hi baby. You sound better. Do you forgive me?"

"I don't know, Carmen. You not telling me you were married, that's a big deal. Let me think on it. Now is not a good time for that conversation. I'll have to call you back. I'm kinda busy right now."

"Busy? Well do you want me to come over tonight so we can talk?"

"No, not really. I have to get ready for tomorrow. I'll just see you at work in the morning, ok?"

There was a brief pause. "Ok. I'll see you in the morning. Maybe I'll stop and get us breakfast."

"That's sweet but I won't have time. I'm in the OR till noon. But we'll talk more tomorrow."

"Ok. If you change your mind, call me. Good night, baby."

"Good night, Carmen." I ended the call. Just as I was putting the phone back into its holster, it rang again. This time it's Lisa.

"Hey Lee-Lee!" She hates when I call her that.

"Don't 'hey' me!" You were supposed to call me back yesterday to tell me how you and Carmen were getting along. What? You couldn't come up for air?"

I couldn't help it. I had to laugh. "I'm sorry Lisa. A lot has been going on. I'm going to have to call you back though. I'm having dinner with Kenya right now."

"Heffa! What the fuck is going on in Atlanta? All weekend you were laid up with Carmen and now you chillin' with Kenya?"

"Long story. I'ma call you first thing in the morning when I'm driving to work."

"Your ass better not call me that damn early in the morning. I know your ass has to be at work for 6 am. I will NOT be your entertainment while you drive. Call me when you get off tomorrow afternoon. And don't make me call Sheila and tell her how you're acting all funny now that you're in Hotlanta."

"Damn, girl. Don't call my momma. I'ma call you tomorrow. Promise."

"Ok. Good night, dimwit."

"Good night, bighead." But Lisa had already hung up. She always beat me to it.

I started to put the phone away but didn't want to deal with Carmen if she called back. I turned the phone off then put it back in its case. Kenya came back to the living room dressed in running shorts and a fitted breast cancer awareness T-shirt. Her bare feet showed a fresh pedicure. "I see you got your dogs done today too, huh?"

She picked up a couch pillow and threw it at me. "Funny. I'll have you know, my feet stay cute, fresh pedi or not."

"I'll take your word for it." I was having fun teasing her.

"Whatever, come in the kitchen and heat up this food while I make the margaritas."

I did as I was told. She pointed me to the silverware and dishes. I made us plates of food and heated them up in the microwave. We didn't talk much for those couple minutes because she was busy mixing margaritas in the blender. "Try it," she said as she passed me a tall, frosted glass. I did. It was delicious.

"Wow, Kenya! That's really good."

"I know," she said with a cocky grin. "Now try my momma's cooking."

That first bite was amazing. The chicken was spicy all right. It wasn't 'burn your mouth out' spicy but it definitely had a kick to it. Overall, the meal tasted like something my mom would make. We talked a bit while eating. Mostly about our families and how we got to where we are in our careers. When we finished eating, I asked the question that had been gnawing at the back of my mind.

"So how do you know Carmen?"

I think she knew that question was coming. She sat up in the chair and became serious. "Carmen and I had a brief fling a few months back. I met her at the club one night. We had sex. Yes, on the same night we met." She said that when she saw my facial expression, which was probably one of complete shock. I guess Carmen had a no holes barred attitude.

"We tried the dating thing but she was still living with that man and had just bought that house. It made no sense to me that she would buy a house with a man she was planning on divorcing. But then I learned that's just who she is. Not saying she's a gold digger, but she's opportunistic. Now that poor guy is stuck in a mortgage . . . Anyway, that's too much info. Long story short, we slept together for a couple months. I didn't know she worked at AGH until Thursday when I went to turn in my paperwork. By then we had already stopped talking."

I was surprised by this new information. Kenya and Carmen had had a thing. Carmen had been in this very condo and then was in mine. And she knew Kenya was my trainee and never mentioned it. Even more interesting was that Carmen bought a house with her husband but knew she was going to divorce him. Did she do that to qualify for the loan? Did he agree to it to try to keep her? Was she really planning on divorcing him?

"Why didn't you know that she worked at AGH?"

"We never discussed it. I knew she was in school for her master's degree but since it was just sex, we never really discussed much of our personal lives. I only knew about the husband because I thought about maybe dating her seriously. I had some flowers sent to her and the delivery guy called me back to tell me some guy had turned him away when he went to her house. I asked her about it and that's what she told me. I ended it then. She tried to explain it to me but it was just too complicated. I still see her out at the clubs but other than a simple hello, I try to pretend she doesn't exist."

"Wow. Why are you telling me all this?'"

"You asked. I figured you wanted to know or you wouldn't have asked."

"I didn't ask about her personal life."

"No, you didn't. But I knew you had found out about him because I overheard your end of the conversation with her a few minutes ago. Guess you forgot my door wasn't all the way closed."

She had valid points there.

"Let's not talk about her right now," I told her.

"No problem. But let me just say, you deserve more than that anyway. Don't let it get you down."

"Do you think she's still sleeping with him?"

"I honestly don't know."

"Ok." We went on to discuss our cases for the next day. We had a few more glasses of Margaritas and before you know it, our conversation went in another direction. By this time we were sitting on the couch facing each other with just the occasional passing car to break up the sound of our voices. We talked about our disastrous dating histories. Ours were quite similar. She was just a year younger than I and was also looking for 'the one.' She wanted a wife and children and felt that as she approached twenty-nine, she was almost out of time.

"I want to have kids, you know? Like actually go through pregnancy and birth them. I want the full experience. And as I get closer to thirty, I get worried about things like Down's syndrome and birth defects and prematurity. It's all so scary. My best friend is a Neonatologist and she tells me all these scary stories about advanced maternal age and what can come as a result. I know it starts at thirty-five but how can I have three kids by then when I don't even have a partner right now?"

"You want three kids? I want four."

"But you say you don't want to give birth?"

"Nope. Not for me."

"Tori, you have this femme/stud thing going on."

"That's what Carmen said. She called me a tweener."

"Yeah, I can see that. Well as you can see, I am all femme. I date aggressive femmes usually."

"Me too. I date femmes. I've dated studs before but it never really worked out."

She giggled. "Yea, I bet. You probably tried to strap them."

"Yep, sure did. You want me to take it but you won't. Puhlease!" We laughed until we both had tears coming from our eyes.

And so our conversation went. She was easy to talk to and I let her know that. I also told her I thought we would be great friends. She invited me to the weekend festivities with her and I told her I would love to. We ended the evening with a friendly hug and I left wanting more. Much more. How had things become so complicated in just the few days I had been a resident of Atlanta.

Kenya

When Tori left, I was left with mixed emotions. I enjoyed her company even more than I thought I would. It was great talking to her. She had a great sense of humor and made the most animated faces when she got excited about something. I didn't want her to leave. I wanted her for myself. I knew I was taking a risk by telling her about

Carmen's situation but she needed to know. Even if she didn't want *me*, she shouldn't be sucked into Carmen's lies.

It was hard for me to sleep that night. I'd been so focused on trying not to like Tori but I was failing at that. I felt so comfortable and at ease around her, but although she's my age, she is my boss and my teacher. How could I cross those boundaries?

8

CHAPTER EIGHT

Tori

On Monday morning, I made it to work a little early because I wanted to make sure I was able to set up my assigned operating room before my first scheduled case. In the locker room, I ran into Kenya. Literally. She was walking out as I was going in and I guess neither of us were paying attention. Her breasts pressed firmly against mine as she stumbled forward and my arms wrapped around her waist to steady her. The physical contact sent a tingle down my spine. A good kind of tingle.

"Tori, girl I am so sorry. I'm a bit hung-over from last night and can't seem to get it together. I came in early to workout in the wellness center. You see that didn't help."

"You need to go home? We can just start tomorrow. I hate that we had all those margaritas yesterday."

"No, I'll be okay. I'm headed to Starbucks to get some coffee. Want some?"

"No thanks. Caffeine is not my friend. I'd be bouncing off the walls. But seriously, if you need to go home, it's okay."

"Girl, I'm a trooper. See you at noon? Maybe we can grab a quick lunch in the cafeteria."

"Probably not today. I need to talk to Carmen. But I'll take a rain check?"

"Sure girl. Handle yours. See you at one." I thought I detected an attitude or slight annoyance. Brushing it off, I started again to walk into the locker room when Carmen came around the corner.

"So you are having margaritas with the spoiled bitch now?"

"Excuse me?" I couldn't believe what I was hearing. "Have you lost your mind?"

"No, Tori. I came here early this morning to try to talk to you and I hear you talking about margaritas with Kenya. Is that why you couldn't answer your phone? Are you sleeping with her now?"

"Carmen, I am not about to get into this with you at work. It's my first day here. It's going to be drama free, whether you like it or not. Now I am going to go into this locker room and get ready for work. You are going to your office and do the same. At lunchtime, I will be by so we can go somewhere and talk *in private*. I don't do workplace drama."

The angry tone in my voice changed her tone. She became apologetic. "Tori, I'm sorry. I guess I got kind of worked up when I heard her talking to you."

"Right now, this conversation is over. I will see you at noon." I didn't wait for her response. I hate walking away in the middle of a conversation but I really don't do workplace drama. She needed to get her shit together or some drastic measures would have to be taken. Not sure what they were, but they'd get the job done.

The rest of the morning went smoothly. I got lost in the OR suites a few times but the nurses and doctors were extremely helpful. By mid morning, I had a nice routine going and felt I could tackle anything. My next case was a major neurosurgery case with Dr. P. Jackson. It never occurred to me that it was Kenya's father.

Dr. Jackson approached me in the holding area and introduced himself as the surgeon for the case. He told me he had heard quite a bit about me from the staff as well as from his daughter. Call me slow, but I still didn't catch on.

Not until he asked me how I liked the food his wife had prepared.

"It was delicious sir. Reminded me of home."

"Good to hear. We are having a cookout on July 4th. The wife and I would love to have you over. It appears you have been quite the talk of the house for some time. My daughter kept going on and on about how her curriculum vitae would look so much more impressive now that she will train under Dr. Becker. Now she goes on and on because Dr. Becker is young and black. You do know how rare that is, right?"

"Yes, sir. And your daughter is making all the right career decisions. The pain management experience will carry her far in pediatric surgery. I'm sure you are very proud of her."

"I am. We both are. She's stubborn like her momma but she's smart."

Laughing, I replied, "Yes, sir. She is definitely stubborn." He laughed too.

That case went well and at noon, I was relieved by one of the other anesthesiologists for lunch. I grabbed a quick sandwich from the cafeteria and headed to the pain clinic.

Carmen was busy signing out a patient when I arrived. She was very professional and courteous. To the outside eye, nothing was out of the ordinary. I took my sandwich into my office and closed the door. I needed a moment of peace before the conversation to come.

There was a chime in the office as the front door opened and closed. *So that's how they know when someone is at the front desk.* I heard shuffling around at the front desk like papers and charts being moved around. I guess that was when the patient left. Another chime sounded and I heard Kenya's voice.

"Good afternoon, Carmen. Is Dr. Becker here?"

"Do you see her here?" she asked with sarcasm and major attitude.

"Look, I don't want any trouble, ok. I will be here the next three months. Let's just call a truce."

"Chic, I don't want a truce with you."

"Carmen, seriously?" I can barely hear Kenya's voice but can detect a change in tone. "Don't let the little fling we had cause any tension. It happened. It didn't work. No biggie."

"I know what your spoiled ass is doing. I'ma tell you right now, that shit ain't flying. Let me see you step to her again . . ."

The statement was cutoff as I walked to the front desk. Carmen was talking with her hands going wild and pointing her finger and Kenya was standing with her hand on her hip. Neither looked happy to see me either.

"Not in this office. This is a place of business. We are professionals and will act as such. Any personal issues need to be left at the door. I don't care what you ladies had in the past, not while I'm within these walls. If there is going to be drama, we can make other working arrangements," I said coolly.

I think they knew I wasn't issuing an empty threat. Both their faces changed to a neutral expression with a hint of embarrassment. Their offensive postures changed as well. I hated pulling out the 'boss card' but the situation was getting out of hand.

In agreement, they both nodded.

"Kenya, why don't you go to the treatment room and get the meds and equipment ready for our first patient."

"Sure, Dr. Becker." She headed to my office. Once she was out of earshot, I turned to Carmen.

"Look Carmen, the situation we have right now is really crazy. I'm just learning about your husband . . ." She started to speak and I continued, "No, let me finish." She became quiet again. "It's not my business what happened in your past unless it affects me. This affects me. I would have appreciated honesty. But at the same time, we haven't known each other that long and so I didn't really give you time to tell me. I would like for us to hang out but I don't think dating would be wise for us at this time. I just want to have fun. Nothing too heavy or serious just yet."

When I was finished speaking, she said, "It's because of *her* isn't it? What did she tell you about me? She's just a hater. Mad because I didn't want her ass."

"No. It's because you are still in a situation. Roommate or otherwise. I don't want to deal with that right now. And we were moving too fast anyway. I just moved here and I really need to take time to enjoy the place and have fun."

"Whatever, Tori. Your loss." I could tell she was upset and wanted to say more but she returned to her paperwork, dismissing me. I took advantage of the opportunity and went back to my office.

It was good to have that conversation out of the way. In two months, it wouldn't matter but for the next two months, I needed to keep the peace with Carmen or things could get ugly at work. Maybe I *was* being judgmental about the situation. But the fact remains; we didn't know each other that well. We just jumped head first into a pseudo-relationship because we were so attracted to each other physically.

I meant what I said to her. I would try to get to know her. Even hang out from time to time. I had spent most of last night deliberating about it and decided to do what was best for my career and me.

Our first patient showed up a few minutes after our talk and we went to work as if nothing had ever happened. Kenya was a quick study. She evaluated the patient's condition and symptoms, formulated a treatment plan, and wrote the prescriptions. I administered the pain block and answered questions. We repeated this for three more patients. It was around 5:00 pm when we wrapped it up.

Kenya, Carmen, and I sat in my office and discussed the cases for the next day. We worked well as a team. If only our relationship outside of work relations could be as easy. Kenya was polite as she said goodbye and left the office.

As soon as the door chimed to signal she was out the door, Carmen locked my office door and came around to my side of the desk, turning my swivel chair to face her. I was a bit caught off guard by this. I wasn't sure if she would bring back up the argument or turn violent. It's not that I thought she could beat me up or anything. After all, I was much taller than her and definitely stronger.

While I contemplated standing in order to better defend myself in case she did decide to lash out, she pulled her scrub shirt over her head and tossed it on the table. "What are you doing Carmen?" I asked quietly.

I thought I had made myself clear in our earlier talk. She didn't respond. Instead her lips curved into a seductive smile as she unclasped her bra and threw that to join her scrub top. Seeing her half-naked in my office was such a turn on, I could not speak. Her pants were off next as she stepped closer to me, straddling my thigh. I could feel the warmth from between her legs as she lowered herself unto my thigh.

I thought about pushing her way, but that was a fleeting thought as she leaned forward to kiss me. I scooted to the edge of the chair and grabbed her voluptuous ass through the thin fabric of her lace panties. Maintaining the kiss, she rocked back and forth on my thigh, moaning and throwing her head back in the process.

I could feel her nails digging into my back as she rode my thigh closer to ecstasy. As she picked up pace and I felt the tension building in her body, I took charge of the moment and raised her hips off my thighs. She opened her glazed eyes in surprise. She was about to cum and I had interrupted her. But I had other things in mind.

I put her to sit on my desk and pulled the panties slowly down her thighs, legs, and then completely off. Knowingly, she spread her thighs and leaned back onto the desk as my lips came into contact with hers, kissing her passionately. My fingers delved into her damp folds, finding and stroking her button. Two fingers walked up and down her inner walls, that muscle clenching and relaxing around them. Her moans turned into groans then turned into screams of pleasure as she came. Her face contorted into an ugly-pretty expression as she whimpered and nibbled on my lower lip.

As horny as I was, I wanted badly to enjoy the moment but the reality of what was happening, finally hit home. How could I expect for Carmen to take my words seriously if I was so quick to give in to her temptations. I sucked in a breath of air and calmed the tingling in the lower part of my body. I was thinking about how to get out of the current situation when the front door chimed. Carmen hurriedly grabbed her clothes but within a couple seconds, there was a knock at my door.

"Tori, I forgot to tell you but I'm making dinner tonight. Was wondering if you'd like to come over." That was Kenya. All the muscles in my body tensed as Carmen, with just her panties and scrub pants on, went to snatch open the door before I could stop her.

Kenya's eyes widened in surprise before Carmen got up close and pointed her finger in her face. "Bitch, this is the last time I am telling you to leave my damn woman alone!"

"CARMEN! That is enough!" I yelled, completely flabbergasted at her outburst and truly embarrassed. "You will *not* disrespect Kenya like that. And like I told you before, we are *not* together. AND, any issues you might have one way or another, will *not* be discussed in *this* manner in *this* place."

My chastising her was not going to be taken lightly. Her response was unexpected. "Tori, your superior behind can kiss my ass. It's okay for you to fuck me on your office desk as soon as that bitch leaves but the minute she shows back up you wanna act all brand new. Well the two of yall bitches can go to hell. I was going to stick it out for the two months but fuck it . . . I QUIT! Don't ever call me again."

Kenya was standing partially in the door way with her mouth wide open and I'm certain my expression was a mirror image of hers. I had broken hearts before and had women mad at me, but none to this extent.

To my horror, Carmen pushed Kenya on her way out the door. I guess Kenya could only maintain her professionalism for so long because her knee-jerk reaction was to push Carmen's small frame the rest of the way out the door.

Then she got in her face and said, "Since you are no longer an employee here, let me tell you something: Disrespect me again and I'm going to show you how much of a bitch I can really be." As Kenya spoke, Carmen took a step back and Kenya's face took on a menacing frown. Even I was scared.

But she continued calmly, "I am a lady first but I *will* whoop your ass. Threaten me again and I will show you what a real threat is. And when you see me out anywhere, you'd be wise to go to the opposite end of the room or cross the street. It's been a long time since I've had to fight a chic but I will if I have to. Don't let the classy appearance fool you."

When Kenya was finished with her warning, Carmen rolled her eyes but said nothing else before she gathered her things and left the office.

I think I was still in shock with the turn of events. I sank into the desk chair and put my face in my hands.

Kenya walked over to my desk and touched my slumped shoulder. She asked, "Are you okay?"

I uttered a noncommittal grunt. She continued, "Are you mad at me?" I snickered at that but shook my head. "You sad that yall broke up?" she inquired. I raised my head and looked her in the eyes.

"No. I'm just upset it turned out like this. So much for no drama in the work place. That's why I don't like to date women from work." Brushing my hair back with my hand, I stood and held the door open for Kenya, signaling to her I was ready to leave. "Thanks for the dinner offer but I think I'm going to have a quick something at home. I've got a headache."

I didn't notice how quiet Kenya was until I was locking up the office. Turning to her I said, "It's not your fault. I'm glad it's over. And look, we'll hang out this weekend at PRIDE."

"Sure. Well, see you tomorrow." Kenya left me standing there. I could detect that things weren't quite okay, but I was still pre-occupied with the evening's events. I couldn't believe I fell to Carmen's seduction. How weak and desperate could I be? Was I really willing to risk my career and ignore my intuition just to find a partner? I knew she was still married. I knew we shared a workspace.

And I knew about the history she and Kenya had. Why did I let things get so far?

And most importantly: How do I explain to the other doctors why Carmen left with no warning? How on earth were we going to find a replacement on such short notice? *Ugh!*

9

CHAPTER NINE

Kenya

I really did go back to the pain clinic to invite Tori to dinner. True, I could have just called her. Of course, I figured Carmen would still be there but it never occurred to me that they would be having sex in the office. Carmen made sure I had no doubts about what they had been doing. I was so angry; I wanted to slap the light-skinned heffa. And I wanted to shake Tori. I wanted her to see Carmen for the manipulative, money hungry, opportunist that she was.

The events that followed were unanticipated. I knew Carmen was from Jamaica and I had heard that Jamaican women were crazy and possessive but I didn't think she would become aggressive like that. After all, the chic couldn't be any taller than 5'2". But she did. And when she did, I snapped. I had to remind myself of my purpose for being here. It wasn't for Carmen or even for Tori. I had come too far to let anyone or anything get in my way.

But I wanted Tori. I realized that last night and knew I couldn't ignore it. I had a decision to make. I could either work my ass off to get these three months over with quickly and move on with my career or I could fight for her. But why fight when it's obvious she doesn't even know I exist.

Sure, she sees me. She speaks to me. She may even flirt with me. But she doesn't really *see* me. I exist only in the literal sense. She doesn't see that I'm crazy about her. She doesn't see what we could be together. And how could I expect her to? We just met a week ago. But I felt like I've known her much longer. I just have to make her *see* me because I'm going to fight for her.

I was so consumed with my thoughts that when I arrived at my car in the parking lot, I didn't notice Jewelle leaning against my car until she spoke. "Well, hello stranger." Even though her voice was low and seductive, she startled me. I think I might have jumped a good three feet back and yelped. She laughed boisterously.

"Not funny, Jewelle. You scared the shit outta me."

"Aaaawww babe, but you should have seen your face." Turning on her charms, she stepped into my personal space and spoke with a sexy lilt, "Although I much rather the faces you were making the other night. Damn, girl. I couldn't stop thinking about you. Had to come see you. Touch you again. Have dinner with me."

Whoa. She wasted no time. And damn if it didn't turn me on. What the hell was I doing? I was just giving myself a pep talk on getting Tori, and now here I was thinking about taking Jewelle up on her offer. But shit, Tori already brushed me off for the evening. Might as well enjoy the company while I have it.

And then it hit me. I was about to fall into the same 'shituation' that Tori did with Carmen. If I wanted to be with Tori, and I mean really wanted to be with her, then all my flings and sexual escapades had to stop right now. No matter that Jewelle was standing here looking sexier than a woman should in a business suit.

As I was deciding my next move, Jewelle ran a nail from her freshly manicured hand down my arm, sending a jolt of electricity up and down my spine and making the decision for me. I wanted the company of a woman tonight.

"I would like nothing better," I finally replied.

Jewelle's smile beamed like a bright light and I could see she really did want to spend time with me. This was more for her than just sex.

"I'm glad to hear that. So will you follow me to my place? I have a brownstone near Lenox Mall and there are a few nice restaurants nearby that deliver."

That would actually work out great. I didn't want to go back to my place and risk running into Tori. "Sure. But all I have to change into are my running shorts and t-shirt. Should I go home first to change?"

"No," she answered with a sneaky grin. "I plan on getting comfortable as soon as I get in anyway."

I followed Jewelle in her white BMW to a small, gated community of four-story brownstones. The security guard at the gate was instructed by Jewelle to hold the gate open for me to enter. We pulled up in her expansive driveway and I admired the landscaping and architecture. The tall brick building looked more like a large house that just happened to be attached to another large home. She had an end unit and the side yard was populated with crepe myrtles of all colors surrounded by lush plantings and encircling a stone bench and small koi pond.

Jewelle met me at my car after parking in her garage, took my hand, and showed me around her "mini" garden. It looked like a scene out of a home and garden magazine. Just beyond the fence gate leading into her backyard, there was a large butterfly bush with lots of colorful butterflies flitting around it. The backyard itself was quite expansive for it to be an attached home. Jewelle answered my thoughts.

"I sold all the homes in this community. There are twenty of them. As a gift, the builder gave me this home. I only paid the taxes. He actually bought it for his girlfriend but his wife found out." We both laughed at that.

"This is absolutely beautiful."

"Thank you. Let's go see inside." She continued holding my hand and a warmth crept through my body. It felt right. But I had to remind myself that this was the same woman who hosted monthly sex parties. She would not be the settling type. She led me back through the gate and to her front door. The large wooden door opened into a three-story foyer. The tan walls reflected the area's light and on further inspection, I realized the tan paint had flecks of metallic gold in it.

"The builder put his all into this property. Everything here is custom." She gave me a tour of the house as if trying to sell it to me. I could see why she was consistently rated as one of the top realtors in the city. She had four bedrooms and four and a half bathrooms. There was a game room and media room, an office, and a workout room. The kitchen had the most beautiful granite countertops and mosaic glass tile backsplash. The center island with breakfast bar, gas cook top with built-in side griddle, and the sub zero refrigerator, were a cook's dream. So I asked, "Do you cook?"

"Yes. About two or three times per week. I love eating out but I prefer a good home cooked meal. What about you?"

"I can cook but my mom usually prepares enough food to last me a whole week. I guess she figures I'm too busy to cook for myself."

"Yes, your mom is a great cook. I had dinner with them a couple years ago. Before your dad bought your condo." I forgot she had met my parents and were actually good friends with them. I hope that didn't complicate things.

She had ordered the food on the way here and the doorbell rang as we finished the tour. I sat at the island while she went and got the food from the delivery guy. She had ordered from a Jamaican restaurant, so we had curry chicken, stew chicken, oxtails, rice and peas, plantains, and coconut tarts and mango ice cream for desert. We decided it was best we showered and got comfortable before we ate. She was quite the lady and showed me to the guest suite where I could get cleaned up in private.

Once I was fresh, clean, and dressed in my shorts and t-shirt, I headed back to the kitchen. She was already there in similar attire. Shorts and a t-shirt that showed off her flat stomach. Her hair still hung in the perfect bob but her face was free of make-up. She looked so much younger without it. And much more beautiful. She caught me staring and raised an eyebrow questioningly.

"What's up?" she asked.

My mother always said I spoke too freely, without thinking, sometimes. "I was just thinking how young you look. How old are you?"

She smiled and didn't seem offended by my observation. "I'm thirty-five. The youthful appearance runs in my family so for work, I wear make-up to help me look more mature. Nobody takes you seriously in my line of work if you look inexperienced. Unfortunately, they use age to gauge experience."

It made sense. It was contrary to what most women try to do, but it allowed her to make a name for herself in the industry. I was liking her more and more.

We ate, talked, and laughed about life in general. After dinner, while sitting on the couch watching The Proposal with Sandra Bullock, she told me she had been living life like Bullock's character. She was so focused on her careers as an agent and nightclub owner -- I was just learning she actually owned the establishment where she hosts her monthly parties -- that she let life slip by and now here she was in her mid-thirties, still single, and no kids. "I used to want at least two children. And now look at me. I don't even have someone I'm dating on a regular."

"Aaawww, Jewelle, I didn't know you wanted kids." Actually, there wasn't much I knew about Jewelle.

"Yea. That's why I wanted this house. The schools around here are great. And the backyard is perfect for a little swing set." She shrugged. "I don't know. I might adopt. I've spoken to an attorney about it. But my life is so busy right now. I can't imagine raising a child on my own. Not now."

Seeing her so open and honest made me want her sexually. Weird huh? Men -- and some women -- hear a woman talking about wanting babies and a family and they run in the opposite direction. I hear it, and I get turned on. Go figure. Either way, I leaned over and kissed her. Although I caught her by surprise, she quickly joined in. She parted her lips for my probing tongue.

The kiss was at first soft and sensual. But desire took over and we acted hungrily. I had her shirt off in record time. She didn't wear a bra so I didn't have to fiddle with that. She managed to get her shorts and thongs off before I could get to them. She helped me with my shirt and shorts and inhaled deeply when she saw I had no panties on.

She was on her knees in front of me in the blink of an eye. Her pink tongue darted from her mouth and with a flick, tickled my clit. That one sudden movement made tears well up in my eyes.

Her soft hands reached behind me to grab my ass cheeks, then pulled me to the edge of the couch. This caused me to fall back and my legs spread automatically. She devoured me. She licked at every drop as if it were the sweetest thing she had ever tasted. Her muffled moans created a humming sensation, a vibration, which brought me to a quick but strong orgasm in just a few minutes.

I helped her up from her knees and laid her on the couch. I parted her legs and slid in between them. Checking to see how wet she was, I slipped one finger in between her folds and stroked her from her outer to inner lips. Using my thumb and index finger, I kneaded her clit.

Once her shrills filled the room, I inserted two fingers into her warm opening letting her juices drip down my fingers with each plunge. She writhed on the couch, raising her hips to meet my hand. I inserted three fingers. Then four. And then my tightly formed fist. Her gyrations increased in frequency and intensity. I lowered my body to hers using my hand as if it were a dick or a strap and I fucked her. When she came, her body shuddered and her juices squirted, landing on my pelvis, mixing with my own juices.

I raised her legs, positioning her knees to her chest and spreading her thighs apart. I balanced myself on my feet and bending at the knees, I lowered myself so my clit met hers. Her wet pussy moved against mine, driving me insane. She called my name repeatedly. "Kenya, Fuck me! Damn, I love you. Kenya. Kenya! Fuck me!" That pushed me over the edge. I rode her for dear life. Just before I came, I opened my eyes to look at her face. She had the prettiest fuck face ever and I saw tears streaming down her face. It was then that I heard the rain. And with tears of guilt escaping my own eyes, I climaxed to the sound of thunder.

10

CHAPTER TEN

Tori

The rest of the week actually went by pretty smoothly.
The doctors in the department just thought Carmen was too
busy with school and getting ready for her new position so
no further questions were asked about her sudden
resignation. They simply pulled in a temp from the nurse
pool.

Luckily, she was a middle aged, white woman who I
was in no way attracted to. She was efficient and thorough
and a definite quick study. We initiated the process of
getting her changed over into a full time position. Martha --
that's her name -- was friendly but professional. A keeper.

Kenya and I were working well together but the
connection that was there before, seemed to have
dissipated. Or at least, lost it's intensity. I should have been

happy for this, but instead, I was wondering what caused her to lose interest. She was nice enough to work with but at the end of the day, she left without any invitations to dinner or any flirtations.

That only made me notice her more. I dreamed about her at night and fantasized about her during the day. I was scheduled to do cases with her father two more days that week. He reminded me of their 4th of July cookout. I was looking forward to the opportunity to spend time with Kenya and her family on her own turf.

During one of those cases, Kenya came in to assist her father. She was cordial enough but seemed focused on the surgery. I sat on my chair writing vital signs and giving drugs. With the blue drapes separating us, I couldn't see Kenya looking at me. Until her father yelled at her to pay attention. I stood in time to make eye contact before she turned back to the monitor. At least I knew I still existed in her eyes.

On Friday, my best friend, Lisa, came from Houston to visit for the weekend. That Saturday was also my thirtieth birthday. Kenya promised to drag us out the house for the

Pride events going on that weekend. I had not been to any of the clubs since moving here and was excited about checking out the scene as well as just being around Kenya.

I picked up Lisa at the airport on Friday afternoon. She was full of energy as usual. I swore she drank coffee by the gallon. "Dimwit!" she yelled across the crowded baggage claim area. I couldn't help but smile. Her 5'1" frame wove through groups of people and she embraced me in a tight hug.

"Hey bighead. If I didn't know better I would think you missed me," I teased. A few tears spilled from her eyes. In all the time I had known Lisa, I had never seen her cry so I was a bit taken aback.

"Of course I miss you. My best friend, practically my only friend, up and moved across the country. What you think?" Then she smiled. "You really are a dimwit." Yup, she was back to her old self. We grabbed her bag and headed to the car.

"Look at my girl riding in style. Sheila said you picked out a nice one but dang!" She was checking out my car.

"I would appreciate it if you didn't call my momma by her first name."

"Tori Becker! Your momma told me to call her Sheila. She also gave me permission to whoop your ass while I'm out here. Now quit being sassy and take me to meet all your women." Our silly banter always ended with her getting the last word. All I could do was laugh with her.

On the ride back to the condo, I filled her in on the latest happening with Carmen and Kenya. "Something about that girl wasn't sitting right with me. From what you told me, she was scheming, possessive, and an obvious gold digger but for whatever reason, you only see the good in people. You better be glad she quit and didn't stick around to ruin your career or jack up your car."

"She's not that kind of person, Lis." I parked the car in my assigned spot.

"Like I said, you only see the good in people." I didn't argue with her because I knew it wouldn't change her mind. And I also knew she was right. She continued, "So Kenya's moved on huh? Guess she got tired of waiting for you to show interest."

Now that took me by surprise. "What makes you think that?" I asked.

"Girl, you are so clueless when it comes to women. She made the first move by interrupting your session with Carmen. You do know she did that on purpose, right?"

"You really think so?" I hadn't thought of it that way. I shrugged it off. "Even if she did do that intentionally, how do you know she moved on?"

"Because she isn't paying you nearly as much attention as she used to. *And* she's getting on the elevator with a very gorgeous woman as we speak." She gestured to the elevator bays. Sure enough, there she was. And the woman with her was quite stunning. I wouldn't admit it to Lisa, but I was jealous.

"How'd you know it was her?" I asked.

"I looked her up on Facebook the minute you told me about her. Do you know she posted about meeting you?"

No, I didn't know about that, but I said nothing, knowing Lisa would continue anyway. "She didn't mention your name or that you were a girl but she said she had met her soul mate."

"Really?" Call me naïve but I didn't think she was that into me. "Whatever girl. She could have been talking about anyone."

Lisa laughed and shrugged. "Ok."

We caught the next elevator. As we entered the condo, my phone rang. It was Kenya. "Hello."

"Hey girl! We still hanging tonight? Did Lisa make it in?"

"Yeah, she's right here." Lisa, realizing who it was and that Kenya asked about her, spoke up.

"Hey, Kenya! Come on over," she yelled into my phone's mouthpiece.

Kenya replied, "Sure give me a minute. Walking my friend to the elevator." And then she hung up without saying bye. These women always have to have the last word.

Ten minutes later, Lisa and I were sitting in the living room having cold beers when the doorbell rang. Lisa bounced off the couch and beat me to the door. When she opened it, she and Kenya hugged as if they had known each other all their lives. I felt like I missed something.

"Girl, it's good to finally meet you. You are even prettier in person." That was Kenya. And I was confused.

"Child hush! Your pics are gorgeous but you in real life . . . you are the hotness!" They hugged and laughed. All the while, I was trying to figure out what was going on.

Seeing how lost I was, Lisa filled me in. "We're Facebook friends. We talk everyday just about."

WTF! "Oh really? About what?" I asked.

"Don't get all pissy acting on me, Tori Lashae Becker!"

"I told you bout using my whole name like that, woman."

"Shut up, dimwit."

Kenya was looking back and forth between us like we were a circus act. Then she burst into laughter.

We sat and talked for a bit before making arrangements to head out that night. "So where are we going?" Lisa asked.

"There's a play downtown. Or we can go to the 25 and over party that my friend is throwing."

"I didn't come all the way to the A-T-L for a play. Let's party. And is this the same chic you just walked out?" Lisa was prying but I wanted to know as well so I sat quietly.

"Yep, that's my friend Jewelle. She's one of the top realtors in the city. She hosts some of the best parties for mature, professional women." Kenya answered unscathed by Lisa's question.

"Hmmmmm. She's hot. She single?" Lisa continued.

"Ummmmm, yeah, I think so. Why, are you interested?" Kenya seemed a bit uncomfortable but I still wasn't saying anything.

"I'm more interested in knowing who my friend has as her competition." Lisa responded with a straight face. I choked on my beer. Kenya tensed.

"Ok, so time to get ready." Lisa said dismissively. She walked to the door and opened it for Kenya. "What time should we be ready?"

Kenya answered softly; obviously trying to regain composure, "Let's aim for eleven."

"Great. I'm really glad to finally meet you. I better start to get ready cause it takes me forever and miss thang over there takes even longer when she tries to looks like a girl."

"Hey!" I spoke up. "I always look like a girl."

"Yes hun, but you don't always look like a girly girl. Tonight you will. Sheila told me to make sure you look like a girl all weekend and send lots of pics."

"Ugh! You and my momma." And turning to Kenya, I said, "Alright Kenya, see you at eleven. I'll drive."

"Ok. See you at eleven."

After closing the door, I turned to confront Lisa but she was already closing the door to the guest bedroom. I guess she knew what was coming. I decided to just use the time to get ready. Besides, she'd get in the last word anyway.

At 11 pm on the dot, my doorbell rang. I was pulling on my heels and grabbing my purse when I heard Lisa letting Kenya in.

"Hey, come in. Sorry about earlier." Lisa apologized sincerely.

"Sorry for what?" Kenya asked, pretending not to know.

"For trying to meddle in your relationship with Tori."

"Tori and I don't have a relationship. She's made it clear that she doesn't want to date me. It's probably for the best anyway. We'd have to work together for years."

"First off, I'm sure Tori didn't tell you she didn't want to date you," Lisa began, and as Kenya began to disagree she said, "Wait, let me finish. She likes you but you're right, she's scared of what would happen to your careers if someone were to find out or if you two didn't work out. Don't write her off just yet."

"I'm seeing someone, Lisa and it's really complicated. Besides, Tori wouldn't want me if she really knew me. All she sees is the surface stuff. I look good on paper but I have trust issues. And I don't have the best history with women and relationships."

"I know about you and your realtor friend. I saw you two holding hands earlier. I'm just saying. Whatever is in your past is in your past. Don't let it block your future. Tori is a wonderful woman. She'll love you till the cows come home."

Kenya laughed, "That sounded really country. Where is she anyway?"

I took that as my cue. "I'm right here."

I heard the sharp intake of breath as I stepped into the living room. Kenya's mouth was hanging wide open. Lisa busted out laughing but managed to say, "Close your mouth girl. You might catch flies."

Poor Kenya. Her face took on a red undertone as she blushed from being called out for blatant lusting. I must say though, I looked damn good. I was wearing a black, strapless, one-piece romper made of a shiny satin material that hugged close to my curves. The legs of the pants ended at mid-calf and I used black strappy stilettos to accentuate my toned calves. The pants hugged my butt and hips nicely so I wore a simple silver pin-on flower at my waist to call attention to that part of my body. The strapless top of the jumper was ornamented with tiny faux diamonds that cast a prism of light across the skin of my upper torso, arms, and neck. My hair was cascading in layers past my shoulders and resting at my shoulder blades. A flat iron went a long way. I finished the look with a diamond necklace, matching tennis bracelet, and stud earrings as well as sassy eye make-up.

"Wow, you look beautiful," Kenya gushed.

"Thank you." I felt beautiful. And confident. I was also admiring Kenya's short strapless dress. It, too, was black and it clung to her curves like another layer of skin. It ended half way down her thigh. Her runner's legs went on for days and ended at silver high-heeled sandals. Her outfit was accessorized with silver jewelry. Her hair was styled similar to mine but was just a bit shorter, showing off her well-defined shoulders. "You look amazing as well."

Lisa grabbed her purse and interrupted our ogling. "Come on chics. Time to party!"

"Lisa," I called to her. "Where are you going in that dress?" Her dress also clung to her body but it had a plunging neckline that showed off her cleavage. She wasn't overly busty, but she wasn't small like me either. She was going to be getting quite a bit of attention tonight.

"I will not be pulling women off of you."

Kenya laughed. I said to her, "No, seriously. I've had to act like her bodyguard a few times. She's so damn tiny so the studs try to step to her aggressively. Especially when she's HALF NAKED."

"I am *not* half naked. Besides, I have my droopy necklace right here. It'll cover up most of the exposed area. Sheesh."

"Just so we're clear." I said as we left the condo.

We rode to the party with the music blasting and trying to sing along. Kenya rode shotgun with Lisa in the backseat enjoying the sights of midtown Atlanta. As we pulled up to a place called the Compound, we valet parked so we wouldn't have to walk far after the party. I knew my feet were going to be hurting and there is nothing cute about a girl limping in stilettos.

The Compound was aptly named. Once inside, there was an expansive outdoor area with intermittent canopy coverage. You could party under the stars. There were several seating areas as well as two large bars, one on either side of the outside area. There was also a pond with a small crossing bridge that led to the bathrooms. The entire area was wall-to-wall women, all dressed in black. We were also dressed in black but it was just coincidence. None of us knew of the theme.

After the outdoor area, there was a large contemporary styled building, which held the enormous dance floor.

Shadow boxes came to life with sexy dancers exhibiting their craft. Go-go dancers, scantily dressed in g-strings and bikini tops, mixed in with the partygoers. Shot girls were selling test-tube shots and some were presenting body shots to eager patrons. The DJ was mixing some dancehall reggae with recent hip-hop. The crowd was live.

We all expressed what a great setup it was. Just as we were ordering drinks at the bar, Kenya's friend, Jewelle, approached us and told the bartender, "Whatever they want is on the house, all night." The bartender gave a nod and went on to making our drinks.

"Thank you," we all said in unison. Kenya introduced us. "Jewelle, this is Dr. Becker. The doctor I'm working with this rotation."

"Dr. Becker, it's nice to meet you," she said with an outstretched hand.

"Like I tell Kenya all the time, please call me Tori. And it's nice to meet you as well." I was nice enough but I think even Jewelle noticed the hint of attitude. What could I say? *I hate you bitch. Go find your own woman.* Nope. Don't think that would have been good. I did manage to shake her hand and I didn't even break it in the process. I turned to introduce her to Lisa but Lisa was nowhere in sight.

I was about to ask Kenya if she saw where Lisa went but got interrupted by a familiar voice.

"Kenyatta Jackson! I haven't seen you in years." The voice exclaimed.

Kenya's response showed her annoyance. "Skye, what the hell do you want?"

"Yes, Skye. What the fuck *do* you want?!" That was Jewelle and judging by her stance, she wasn't very happy.

"I want to talk to the only woman I've ever loved" Skye responded boldly.

"Bitch, I hired you to emcee my party. *Not* to hit on my woman." By now Jewelle was yelling, Kenya was standing with her eyes and mouth wide open, Lisa was back by my side, and I was totally lost.

Oh shit!

11

Chapter eleven

Kenya

It's amazing how all shit can hit the fan at the same time. I was in shock. Traumatized even. I hadn't seen or spoken to Skye in quite some time. Not since the break up. I knew she DJ'd but it never occurred to be that I could run into her at Pride. After all, in these last 10 years, the most I had seen or heard her was on billboard ads and on her morning show. I saw her at a few parties but I steered clear, most of the time, leaving after a few minutes. Even then, to me, she was just Rainbow Skye. It wasn't the Skye I once knew.

Now, her beauty was accentuated by her long, neat locks which had a tint of copper color to a select few, a small diamond stud in her nose, and three piercings in each ear. Her jeans hung low on her hips and a fitted t-shirt showed off her flat stomach. A diamond-laced hoop pierced her bell button and a rainbow tattoo hung like a canopy above it.

Her light brown skin glistened under the club's spotlights. She wore eyeliner and a smoky eye shadow giving her a mysterious look. Her bright brown eyes took in all of me, examining me as if she had never seen me before. Her staring was irritating me.

Before I could speak, Lisa spoke for me. "Kenya doesn't want to speak to you." The little woman had both hands on her hips and had stepped in front of me as if protecting me. Tori was standing immediately behind me and put her hand on my shoulder. My girls had my back.

"What are you? Her spokesperson? She can speak for herself." The chic had some nerve.

"Yes I can, and I'm telling you I don't want to speak to you." My voice was low, shaky, but that was from the building adrenaline. Too much excitement in one night.

"Oh, so because you're a doctor now, you want to act all brand new. Even as a doctor you could never make what I do!" Skye was yelling, trying to belittle me in public to cover her embarrassment. I knew the routine. Had been here before with other women I had rejected for one reason or another. But this time, I didn't need to react or defend myself. My knight in shining armor -- and her petite accomplice -- stepped right in.

"Rainbow Skye, I love your show. It's quite entertaining. And your voice was made for radio. That's why I'm going to give you the chance to walk away before I beat your ass so bad you won't be able to speak through the fat busted lip I'll give you."

I had never heard Tori speak of violence. Just never imagined she could hurt a fly, much less a human being. But she was within inches of Skye now and by the look on her face and her fists clenched at her side, she meant every word of that threat.

Skye looked Tori up and down and laughed. I guess she assumed since Tori looked very feminine tonight, that she was talking hot air. She took the small step that put her and Tori face to face. "What you say, bitch? You tryna jump bad in front of your owner?"

In a blink of an eye Tori stepped out of her high-heeled sandals, pulled back her arm, and punched Skye dead in the mouth. Skye was caught off guard by the blow. You could tell she didn't expect Tori to carry through. Lisa pulled me aside and told me "You might want to step back. Tori's about to kick her ass."

I couldn't let Tori fight my battle. As chivalrous as that was, I didn't want her to risk getting charged with assault and battery and subsequently, having her medical license put on suspension. I charged in between the two, looking to stop the fight. But it had already ended. Maria, the girl I had the threesome with at Jewelle's party, had restrained Skye and was leading her out the door. Apparently, Maria was working security tonight. She winked at me as she passed by, pushing through the newly formed crowd.

Seeing the mini-duel was over, the people dispersed. I ran to Tori to look at her hand. She was shaking it as if to shake the pain away. The skin had broken around her knuckles and blood was pooling at the site of the wounds. She was definitely going to need stitches.

Conveniently, Jewelle rejoined our group. She hugged me. "Baby, are you okay?" she asked, feinting concern.

"I'm fine Jewelle. But Kenya has busted up her knuckles. I'm going to take her home and stitch her up."

"Why don't you just let them go to the ER?"

"Because they are going to want to know how it happened. She doesn't need the type of attention that would bring," I answered impatiently.

"Well don't you think you should stay here and support me? I am hosting a party."

"You seriously think your party is more important than my friend's busted knuckles? The same friend that stood up for me when you disappeared?"

"I didn't disappear. I went to get Maria to keep things in check. How was I supposed to know your little friend was going to get ghetto. Aren't doctors supposed to be refined? Classy?" Her sarcasm was ringing loud and clear. But again, before I could answer, Lisa spoke up.

"Ghetto? Really? Cause where we come from, we call that defending your woman."

"Except, that's not her woman. Kenya and *I* are together," she replied.

"Uh, no the hell we aren't. I already told you. I know the type of lifestyle you live. That's not what I want," I answered.

"You weren't saying that last weekend when you fucked me and Maria. AT THE SAME DAMN TIME!" she hissed at me.

I could hear Lisa and Tori gasp. I was really embarrassed but more pissed at being called out like that. My first thought was to slap her but I figured we'd had enough violence for one night. Instead, I countered, "You're right. But where as I did that one time for the heck of doing it, that's how you live. Maria told me you guys are together.

Have been together for years. You want somebody to invite into your relationship permanently. You think she's okay with it but she's not. We had lunch this afternoon and she explained it all to me. She even told me how you got my father to tell you how badly I want kids and a family. The things I like to do. Where I work. What I'm trying to do with my life. She said you were a lying, sneaky, person that would do whatever it took to get what you want. So before you try to check me, check yourself." While her mouth was still hanging open and smoke was coming from her ears, I grabbed Tori and Lisa's hands and headed for the exit.

At the door, Maria stopped us and said, "She set all that up with Rainbow Skye. She wanted to be the one to run up and save you but by using me as security to break things up. She didn't know your friend would punch the shit out of her before I got there. Skye talks shit but she's a lot softer than she used to be back in the day. She wasn't going to really do anything to your friend. Sorry it came to this, but like I told you, she'd do anything to get what she wants."

"Thanks Maria. Are you going to get in trouble for telling me all this?"

"I'm running security at Jewelle's events. I carry a gun wherever I go. Sometimes two. I'm ex-military and did some martial arts and hand to hand combat training. Jewelle can't even kill a bug without me there to hold her hand. No. The most she'll do is dump me but at this point, I don't care. She'll come back after a week. Nobody else will put up with her lifestyle. I love her and she loves me."

I could here Lisa snicker behind me. Guess she agreed with me that Maria and Jewelle were both crazy and full of shit. Glad I'd dodged that bullet, I said goodbye to Maria and we headed to the car.

I really wasn't that into Jewelle to begin with. She was a very sexy distraction to help me get over Tori. It wasn't very successful. I spent a lot of time talking about work and the 'wonderful' Dr. Becker. Unfortunately, I slipped up a few times and spoke of her casually, referencing her as 'Tori.' Jewelle inquired about it but I refused to divulge any extra information. I do believe it would be quite tacky to tell the girl I am sleeping with about the girl I am in love with. Don't you think?

Maria and I met for lunch this afternoon at the hospital's food court. She had contacted me the night before saying she had something to tell me. I was a bit nervous about seeing her, thinking maybe she wanted us to 'hook-up' again. I was already thinking about ending my fling with Jewelle and really didn't want to add to an already immoral situation. I prepared myself to tell her "Hell no." I mean, Maria was as sexy as they came, and the sex had been memorable, but I wanted to wipe the board clean and wait for Tori.

At lunch, she filled me in. Apparently, her and Jewelle had met, ironically, at a strip club where Maria danced. Jewelle was just starting up her party business and was looking for 'servants'. The pay was much better than where she was working at the time so she took the job. She knew what the duties were but it was no worse than what she had been doing at the club, except this had better clientele and was way more discreet.

They hooked up that first night, and had been together ever since. Maria didn't live with Jewelle but had plans to move in as soon as Jewelle allowed her to do so. For now, Jewelle put her up in a cute condo in Buckhead. She knew Jewelle had a healthy, variable sexual appetite. While they had one on one sex regularly, Jewelle often invited other women to join them. Maria didn't like it but she did what she could to ensure a long lasting relationship.

Lately, Jewelle had been talking about wanting to invite someone to join the relationship, permanently. She said if Maria was going to move in, then their occasional trysts will probably end and she needed more than one woman to satisfy her. That's where I came in.

My father, in his attempt at finding me a new home, had mentioned me to Jewelle. He told her of my wanting to move to the suburbs and starting a family. But he also told her he wasn't sure how I would do that, given my lifestyle. I was a marked woman after that.

I must give it to her. Jewelle had it all planned out. She was trying to create a powerhouse. A top-selling Realtor, an attorney, and a surgeon. The house was certainly big enough for all of us and the kids she wanted to adopt. But I wasn't having it.

The story, although farfetched, was backed up by video footage from a hidden camera Jewelle had placed. She recorded our intimate moments for Maria to try to convince her I was the right one. Maria showed me a few of the videos. I was livid.

I developed a plan to record a similar video in my own home and blackmail Jewelle with it. If I blacked out my face, I could show it to the Atlanta Realtor's Association and she would lose their support. I knew Jewelle would do anything to prevent that. Including giving me all the videos she had with me in them. I hadn't fine-tuned my plan as yet, but I won't need to now. Tonight ended whatever shot I had of getting those videos back. I could only hope she wouldn't put me on blast. But something told me she would.

12

CHAPTER TWELVE

Tori

What a crazy night. I was still trying to put the pieces together as we got into my car. My knuckles throbbed from the contact with Skye's face so Kenya volunteered to drive. As we pulled into my parking space, she finally spoke.

"I am so sorry for ruining your night. I know you have lots of questions and I'll answer them all. Just, please don't let this mess up your whole weekend."

"I do have questions, but we don't have to discuss it tonight. As far as the weekend goes, it's only just begun. Lisa had mentioned earlier about wanting to visit the strip club so we might head out there after you bandage up my hand. Wanna come?"

Her face lit up. I could tell she was relieved I would be cool about the situation. To the outsider, I might seem stupid or naïve but really, I was just picking my battles. I wasn't sure about the events that occurred in her past, but what I *do* know is that it's in the *past*. The opportunity to get with Kenya presented itself again and I was not going to let it slide by me again.

She agreed to come to the club with us. She stitched up my knuckles with a suture kit she had in her condo and we all changed into more comfortable clothing. I donned a pair of boy's skinny jeans, a fitted t-shirt that said "Trust me, I've done this before", and a pair of Chuck's. Lisa came out rocking a cute summer romper that came a few inches below her butt cheek. And Kenya – Kenya wore a sleeveless one-piece short set made of a light khaki material. The thin fabric hung loosely but still managed to cling to her body in the right areas. I shook my head to clear it of the images my imagination had conjured.

On the way out the door, I grabbed a scrunchie and pulled my hair into a ponytail. Lisa commented. "I'ma tell Sheila you dressed like a boy."

"Do that and I'll tell her you dragged me out to a strip club," I countered.

"Damn. Alright, alright."

Kenya laughed at our antics.

We arrived at Strokers and the parking lot was still packed at 1:30 am. Located in Clarkston, GA, it was one of the best gentleman's clubs in the Atlanta Metro area. I had visited a few others in my earlier travels during Black Pride and various medical conferences but Strokers was, by far, my favorite. I liked them because most of the women were amazingly beautiful and had banging bodies. They also had a little bit of everything for everybody. From slim to thick. Small to voluptuous breasts. Moderate ass to a ridiculous amount. And everybody knows, I love ass!

I was very excited to see the girls but even more so to spend time with Kenya and my #1 hang buddy. Lisa was about as cuckoo about ass as I was. As we paid the entrance fee, she asked the chic at the door for "one hundred 'ones'". I already knew what time it was. Kenya and I did the same. We found seats near the other women in the club.

Strokers was sexually integrated, yet lines of definition still existed. As you first enter, closer to the main stage, women, obviously lesbian, occupied tables. That was approximately one-third of the crowd. Then in the middle, as you worked your way to the back, there were tables with male and female patrons. It appeared they were couples and a few guys picking up bisexual women. In the very back were the guys flying solo or with other guys enjoying the scenery. There were a few smaller platforms back there for private dances.

Once we found seats, the waitress came and took our drink order. We chit chatted and each picked out two girls we wanted to get dances from. As I was watching one girl walk by, my eyes glimpsed a familiar face.

I tapped Kenya and asked, "Is that Carmen?" Lisa's nosy ass spun around in her seat so quick.

"Where?" she asked, obviously anxious to see the woman who tried to claim me.

Kenya turned around to verify my sighting. "Yep. That's the heffa." Her and Lisa laughed. I was too nervous to join in. Instead, I asked, "Who's she with? Is that her husband?"

Kenya answered. "No. Don't think so. Are you jealous?"

I replied, "No."

And Lisa added to her, "Are you?"

Kenya was put on the spot and apparently, didn't like it so she took the opportunity to go tip the dancers on the main platform. I watched her try to appear unmoved by Lisa's question but I could see her shoulder's slump just a little.

"Lisa, why'd you do that? She's already had a rough night."

"Because she needs to admit to herself that she really does have feelings for you. You should be thanking me. My advice doesn't come for free."

"Whatever. So you think even after all that she's been doing with Maria and Jewelle, that she wants me? And not to mention she's dated Miss Celebrity herself, Rainbow Skye."

"If she wanted either of them, she'd be at the club right now. Not here with you. Why are you doubting this?"

I thought about it before answering. "I guess at first, it was because she's my trainee and the rules at the hospital say attendings can't date trainees."

Lisa interrupted. "But that hasn't stopped you in the past. I clearly remember you dating at least two of your attendings. And quite a few nurses."

I had to laugh at that one. She was right. During my residency and fellowship, I had a brief rendezvous with a married attending physician and had been in a one-year relationship with another. It was also against the rules in the Houston Hospital System but I did it anyway.

"But the big difference is, now *I* am the attending. I don't want to lose my job for something that may not even work out. And I'm sure she doesn't want to risk hers either."

I love Lisa. She's always to the point, straight up, no chaser. "Heffa, last I checked, Kenyatta Jackson was grown. If she wants to risk it, then who the hell are you to stop her? And wouldn't it be worth it all if you found true love? That's all you've been talking about since you turned twenty-nine. Now the possibility of finding it is right in front of you and you want to play the punk role. It's a wonder the girl is even interested in you still after the shit you pulled with Carmen. Man up!"

She gave me food for thought. Who would have thought the strip club would be a good place for a therapy session?

Kenya came back to the table and scooted her chair close to mine. She put her arm around the back of my chair and played with my ponytail. My breath caught in my throat. Lisa laughed raucously at my obvious surprise. When I turned to look at Kenya, she smiled at me, and then said to Lisa, "Yes, I'm jealous." That made me blush and made Lisa grin like the Cheshire cat.

Kenya stayed close at my side while our private dances commenced. It seemed we all had similar taste as far as ass went. We picked out a total of seven girls. We each had

two selections, and then one that we picked out together.
There were light skinned girls, dark skinned girls, medium
brown girls. Some with glasses, some with colored
contacts. Some with long weaves and others with short
cuts. Piercings and tattoos were varied, as were the
different entertaining tricks.

One girl could fold her legs behind her shoulders.
Another did the entire dance on her head. My favorite was
the girl who could make her booty clap so loud, you could
hear it across the room. Lisa's was a dark skinned girl with
the prettiest ass. Her trick was, she could fold money with
her coochie lips and then make her pussy vibrate which
also made the money do funny dances and flips. Kenya
liked the petite dancer that could make her booty bounce,
twirl, and pop without moving any other part of her body.

When the dances were over, we took shots from the
shot girls. They also had tricks up their sleeves. The first
took the test tube filled with the colorful liquid and sucked,
licked, and deep throated it like it was a dick, then turned
tipped it upside down so Lisa could take a drink. The next
used her breasts to pass the drink over to Kenya's lips. The
last girl flipped upside down on her head, inserted the test
tube into her pussy and told me to reach down and take it
with my mouth. My eyes bugged out my head. I didn't

even have to answer, Kenya told her, "No, thank you." We all laughed when the girl left.

"She was bold," I said.

"Naw, she was nasty,'' Kenya replied.

"Naw, that was hot. Will have to try that some time," Lisa's freaky behind chimed in. We all laughed.

After a few more drinks and several other sets, I excused myself and went to the bathroom. Passing the bar, I felt a small hand grab my ass. It was the shot girl. She winked at me. I smiled nervously then hurried away.

There were two stalls in the bathroom. One was occupied by two women who were either well acquainted or getting to know each other, as evidenced by the sounds of lips smacking and moans. I quickly used the other stall and as I was washing my hands, the two women stepped out. One was the stripper that did the trick with the money using her coochie muscles. The other was Carmen.

By the look on her face, she was surprised to see me standing there. I guess she didn't spot me earlier. I wiped my hands and started for the bathroom door but she grabbed my hand to stop me. "I didn't expect to see you here. It's not what you think."

I decided to play dumb. "What's not like I think?" I asked.

"This isn't what it looks like."

The door had squeaked open and Kenya stepped in. I could tell she was angry. "Why is it that cheaters, liars, dogs, and hoes all say the same thing? Is that yall's motto? What it looks like is that you just came out the bathroom stall of a strip club with another woman who happens to be a stripper, after just sitting on a man's lap in the audience. Did I miss anything?" Kenya's tone said she wasn't up for shit. But Carmen tried her anyway.

"Kenya, don't act like a saint. In case you forgot to tell Miss Tori here, you've had one relationship. One. The rest of the time, you were a self-admitted hoe. Before you get to pointing fingers, tell Dr. Becker what a nasty, trifling, scandalous trick you are."

The stripper took that as her cue to leave and I took that as my cue to step in between the two of them. I faced Kenya to tell her, "She's not worth it. Just let it go, babe." I thought I saw her jaw muscles relax and her shoulders definitely did, but Carmen just *had* to egg her on.

"I was worth it when you fucked me in your office, in your bed, and in your brand new car. Oh and Kenya, wasn't I worth it when your pitifully desperate ass sent me those flowers asking to be with me? Your hoeish ass thought I would settle for you. Bitch please. Now your father, him

I'd fuck so hard he'd leave your momma. You never know, might have done it already."

Carmen pushed past me and headed to the door. But Kenya stepped in her path. Before I could stop her, Kenya's hand met Carmen's face with a loud crack that sounded like thunder. Carmen gasped and grabbed her face, but the look Kenya gave her made her think twice about hitting back. Then, Kenya just turned calmly and walked out of the bathroom.

I was in shock for a few seconds but I ran to catch up to Kenya. I grabbed her hand, steering her out of the club. I mouthed, *"We'll be right back"* to Lisa on the way out. I held Kenya's hand even while we were outside. I could see she was still upset but she said nothing.

"Kenya, you can't go around slapping people because they say stupid shit."

"You just popped Skye in the mouth a couple hours ago. Do you really want to go there?"

I had to laugh. She had a point.

"Okay, I was wrong too. But we can't both be going around assaulting people. Who's going to bail us out of jail?" That got a laugh out of her. Even though the evening was hot, she snuggled closer to me, gave me a hug, then a quick peck on the cheek. We stood outside, silent, for about five minutes.

"I'm good now," she assured me with a smile.

I felt closer to Kenya as we walked hand in hand back into the club. We noticed Lisa was no longer sitting by herself. In fact, there were two studs sitting with her, one actively caressing her back. My instinctive nature to protect her had me tugging Kenya along quickly, weaving through the crowd. When we got to the table, I had to do a double take.

It was Toya, who we call Toy, Lisa's girlfriend of four years. The other stud was Andrea, who we all called Dru. They were my best friends.

"Oh my gosh!" I exclaimed, completely surprised but so happy to see them. "What the hell are you guys doing here? When did you get here? How did you get here? How'd you know where we were?" I asked hurriedly.

The whole group laughed while I blabbered on. Dru and Toy both hugged me while Lisa dabbed at her.

"We came to celebrate with you," Toy answered.

Toy, Dru, and Lisa were my best friends. Lisa was the connection otherwise we probably would not have become friends. You know how we lesbians loved to form friendship with our exes and the exes of our exes? It was sort of like that. After Lisa and Toy got back together, they introduced me to Dru. It was the only way Toy could feel comfortable with Lisa and I remaining friends. She needed to see me with other people. Who better than her best friend?

Dru and I dated for a few months. But once she saw I was more on the aggressive side, she bailed and ran back to *her* ex. It hurt because I was really digging her but I was also glad because Dru had some serious commitment issues. Or so, I'd been told. Even still, if I hadn't relocated to Atlanta, I would probably still be crushing on her.

Both Toy and Dru were shorties. Toy was shorter at 5'2, so she and Lisa made the perfect couple. She had a slim athletic build and an impressionable smile. Dru was slightly taller at 5'4. She was slightly thicker than Toy but still slim. She hid her curves under boyish clothes but neither of them did the baggy thug look. They were soft studs. Toy wore a short, boy cut but her full lips and bone structure revealed her softer side. Dru wore here hair in a cute wrapped bob.

After Dru and I parted ways, I harbored some anger towards her, but after a couple months, the four of us started hanging out like we used to. We were inseparable. It was so hard to leave them behind in Houston.

"We couldn't miss your birthday. Not the big three-O!" Dru yelled above the music in the club. Meanwhile, Kenya motioned to the DJ and he gave her a nod. I was about to ask her what that was all about, when, out of the corner of my eye, I saw several of the dancers coming my way. The music scratched and Uncle Luke's Birthday Song replaced it. I realized what was going on and broke into a blush and grin.

"I'ma kill yall!" I yelled to my friends. But they knew I would enjoy my gift. Thirty women surrounded me in varying phases of nudity. Within thirty seconds they were all naked. I was alone in a sea of bodacious ass and I couldn't be happier. My best friends, a beautiful woman, and ass all around me. What a way to bring in my thirtieth birthday.

13

CHAPTER THIRTEEN

Kenya

It was after four in the morning when we finally made it home. What started out as a not so great evening, turned out pretty good if I do say so myself. Lisa and I had been concocting this evening for a few days and in such a short time, we managed to pull it all together. Tori appeared to have had a blast at Strokers and there was more to come. The issue at hand was the sleeping arrangements. Lisa made the final decision on that.

"Kenya, do you mind if Tori crashes at your place? Dru will take her room and Toy and I will stay in the guest room. Would hate to put her butt on the couch."

I saw Toy pinch her, probably embarrassed by her boldness, but I'd grown accustomed to Lisa's straight to the point attitude. I don't think I would be surprised by anything else she said.

"Sure, not a problem," I replied. "Tori, you wanna grab some stuff?"

Tori had the biggest smile on her face. I wasn't sure if it was my response or the effects of the Hennessey that did it. Either way, I was happy to see her happy. She nodded and went to her room to throw some things in a bag. Lisa approached me and pulled me into the kitchen.

"Thanks for helping to make her birthday special. Because I like you and want to see you two together, I'm going to give you a few hints. Is that okay?" she asked.

"Ummm, sure. You don't have to ask. You haven't *been* asking." We both laughed at that because she knew it was true. Lisa didn't need permission to speak. She did so without hesitation. This must be really important.

"Alright. First, don't bring up anything that happened with Jewelle or Maria. Let her ask you about it. When she's ready to hear it, she will let you know. If you push it on her, she'll get irritated and block you out completely." I nodded my understanding. She continued, "Second, go with the flow. If she wants to sleep in the guest bedroom, let her. If she wants to sleep in your room, as long as you're comfortable, let her. I can't feel her out right now to see exactly where her head is so you just have to go with the flow. *But*, and this is third, under no circumstances should you sleep with her within the next couple of weeks."

Seeing my confusion, she expounded. "I know I said go with the flow, but trust me on this. Tori thinks you're hot. But if she thinks you're easy, especially under the circumstances that occurred this evening, she won't take you seriously. That's where Carmen went wrong. Tori will try you but you gotta resist. Let her work for it. I know she really likes you and I think you might be the one for her, that's why I'm sharing all this. Now in the words of Ru Paul, 'Don't fuck it up!'"

Her final words lightened the tone of her warning but the message still rang clear. I appreciated the advice and let her know it. It might me tough to resist Tori, especially if she kept switching up her style on me. I loved the way she flipped from femme to soft stud. Versatility was such a turn on. And it helped that she was self-sufficient, smart, and family-oriented. On paper, she was exactly what I had been praying for. But the biggest obstacle still remained. Was she worth the risk of losing my job?

Tori emerged from her room with a duffle bag. Toy and Dru looked at Lisa and started laughing. They must have known what she was about to say. "Heffa, you moving out? Shit, you just going two doors down."

Tori blushed slightly but kept on smiling. That Hennessey must have really taken effect. She just took my hand and led me to the door. We bid everyone good night and Lisa winked at me. Tori opened the door for me but went right back to holding my hand.

At my door, she took my keys and opened the door for me. She closed the door after her, and as I continued into the open area, she pulled me to her and kissed me full on the lips. It started as a slow, soft kiss, but progressed to a deep, passionate kiss, her tongue penetrating my mouth and mating with mine. Her mouth tasted like Werther's caramel candies with a hint of Listerine. Guess the Werther's was to cover up the taste of the Listerine. I wouldn't have cared either way.

Her arms enveloped me as she pulled me even closer. My hands, working on a mind of their own, released her ponytail and my fingers went quickly to the task of massaging her scalp. A soft moan escaped her lips and I felt her heartbeat quicken against my chest. Her hands traveled south to cup my ass and I felt my lower parts secrete their potion. I wanted nothing more than to take this all the way, but Lisa's words lingered fresh in my mind and I broke the kiss.

Tori's eyes sprung open at the loss of contact and I answered her unspoken question. "Let's take our time. Get to know each other. See if this is what we really want." The puzzled expression transformed into one of understanding which then allowed for the return of her smile. Her eyes brightened as she led me to the couch.

"Fine," she said, "Let's get to know each other."

We talked until the sun came up. Literally. It was about eight o'clock when Lisa knocked at the door. Tori answered it. We had just laid out on the sectional sofa and covered up with blankets so I was in no mood to move. Lisa entered but said nothing. Tori finally said, "What do you want, Lisa?"

"Don't give me attitude, Tori Becker. Kenya, I thought we had an itinerary to stick to?" she asked.

And then I remembered. "Oh shit, Lisa! I am so sorry. I'll jump in the shower and then we can head out."

Tori's puzzled face was so cute, I paused to kiss her before I ran into the bathroom. I heard her questioning Lisa about what was going on but Lisa shut her up instantly. Whatever courses she took on how to keep women in check, I needed to take the same ones.

I had just stepped into the shower when I heard the bathroom door open. I hurriedly tried to wash the soap off my face but Tori stepped into the shower before I had time to stop her. Her sleepy eyes were filled with lust. My eyes took in the full length of her. She hid her hips well under clothes. Here in front of me, I was able to fully appreciate what clothes did no justice to. Her small breasts were so perky and the tiny nipples called to me. All she had to do was touch me and Lisa's warning would be out the window. Fortunately, she was sticking to my wishes.

"Don't worry. I just wanted to shower with you. I won't touch you. Unless, of course, you want me to." Her crooked grin and one eyebrow raised was enough to break the tension. We laughed. Two women, highly attracted to one another, showering after a night of serious alcohol consumption, and the only thing we did was look at each other and kiss occasionally. Impressive, I must say.

She even helped me lotion my back without trying to grope me, although I could tell it was hard for her. Instead she focused on Lisa's secret mission. It seemed Miss Tori was not fond of surprises. She always had to be in control. But not this weekend.

She interrogated me, even using her fingertips to massage my neck and shoulders, trying to milk the answers out of me. The only thing she managed to get was longer, deeper kisses that made it hard for us to refrain from tearing our clothes off.

"The only thing I can tell you is you and the bois are hanging out today while Lisa and I run some errands. We'll meet you guys for brunch at noon but then we have to head back out. Have you been to Gladys Knight and Ron Winan Chicken & Waffles in Midtown?"

"No," she answered with a pout.

"Sorry, Tori but that's all I can tell you. I gotta run but I'll see you at noon, ok? And don't worry, you'll love your surprises." I grabbed my keys and hurried to meet Lisa. She was at the door about to knock when I opened it.

"Sorry, Lisa. We stayed up all night talking. I took your advice," I told her.

"Good. How'd it go? Did she bring up Jewelle and Maria?"

"No. She said she didn't want to talk about it. As long as it didn't happen while her and I are trying to build something." I shrugged as we rode the elevator to the parking deck. "It's her prerogative, right?"

"Yep. She's a big girl. So yall are going to try?"

"Yes, but we still haven't talked about how it would affect us at work. I guess we'll just keep things quiet and see how it goes. But you know, she did ask about Skye and I. She wanted to know why we broke up." I proceeded to tell Lisa about my past relationship with Skye and my trust issues when it came to dating women. By the time I was finished, we were at our destination. We handled the tasks at hand before heading to Midtown to meet the bois.

Gladys Knight's was packed as usual but lucky for us, we made reservations days before. Lisa was a little upset because Tori, Dru, and Toy were not there when we got there. It was 11:45. I had to remind her that she told them to meet us at noon. Lisa had some serious drill sergeant tendencies. From what I could see, she was meticulous when it came to attention to detail and time.

Promptly at noon, the three Stooges arrived and came to the table laughing. Toy tried to kiss Lisa but she turned to give her cheek instead of lips. That made the three of them laugh even harder. The way Lisa was looking, I would be afraid if I was in their shoes.

Tori spoke first. "We knew you would be mad if we came at twelve. If you wanted us here at 11:45, why didn't you just say that, woman?" Again, laughter from the other two Stooges.

"Whatever Tori. Don't act brand new because it's your birthday. You know I'll jump across this table at you." That shut them up. Lisa smiled. "Now time for your next surprise, dimwit."

I was nervous and I could see Toy fidgeting in her seat. Dru had a silly grin on her face. She was enjoying all of this.

"Ok, don't keep me waiting. What is it?" Tori asked, looking around the room and under the table for a buried gift.

"I got a job!" Lisa announced. Tori looked at her like she was crazy.

"That's my surprise? You got a job? You've had a job. But congratulations, I guess." The four of us that understood what she meant, laughed.

Lisa corrected, "Sorry, I'm so excited I can't even get my words out right. I got a job *here*. In Atlanta. I'm going to be doing therapy for the Atlanta Talons. I signed the contract today. That's where Kenya and I went this morning. We're moving to Atlanta. All of us!" Her voice raised one octave as she told the news. Meanwhile, Tori's eyes bugged out of her head before she started crying.

"You fucking kidding me?!" she exclaimed. "Don't play with me like that Lisa."

"I'm dead serious. We start in October when the Talons' contract expires with their current rehab group. And on Monday before we fly back home, I have an appointment. That's the other part of the surprise. Toy and I are going to try to get pregnant! We're going to see Kenya's perinatologist friend on Monday to see if we can do in vitro fertilization."

"What the hell? Ok, quit playing."

Toy spoke up. "She's not playing. Dru and I pitched the deal to the manager of the Talons a few months ago about the three of us providing Sports Medicine services to the team. They liked our proposal but since Lisa's the one with the actual degree in physical therapy, they wanted to speak to her directly. We'll continue the promoting and business management side like we were doing in Houston. She even gets to hire two assistants. And the baby thing, well you know she's been wanting to do that for forever.

They are okay with it as long as she has the two assistants to help her out while she's out on maternity leave."

By this time, Tori was speechless, mouth wide open, and tears threatened to fall. I squeezed her hand under the table. She smiled at me then gave each of her friends a hug. "This is amazing! I'll have my crew with me here in Atlanta. I'ma be an auntie. Wow."

Lisa teared up too, as they hugged. Me, being the mush that I am, joined in. Toy and Dru looked like they would shed a tear or two but they held it together.

"We're going to look for a house in Decatur, Stone Mountain, Lithonia, maybe even Conyers or Covington. We want the yard space for the baby to play. Dru did you decide where you wanted to live? Is Sasha coming?" Lisa asked.

Dru's shoulder became rigid but her tone was nonchalant, "I doubt it. Things aren't going too well. She doesn't like that we are moving here after Tori did. She thinks I'm following her."

"Well in essence, you are, but not for the reasons she's thinking. We are the Three Amigos. The Three Musketeers. We do better when we're together. And this was an opportunity we couldn't pass up. You could finish your physical therapy degree while handling the PR portion of the company. And we already have a five-year contract with the Talons. She's just an evil, selfish . . ." Toy's ranting was interrupted by the waiter. Thank goodness. I didn't like where the conversation was headed.

Ok, so from what I gathered, Tori and Dru were once an item and her girlfriend didn't approve of them remaining friends. Toy obviously didn't care much for Sasha. Lisa did not mention that to me. The four of them had an interesting dynamic. They seemed to know each other inside and out. And I was feeling *left out.*

I wasn't entirely uncomfortable with the revelation but I resigned myself to accept it. Tori built her circle of friends before I met her. How could I dare try to change that? I needed to trust that her and Lisa and her and Dru would never revert to being bed buddies. Trust goes a long way in a relationship.

After the meal, the bois headed to the mall and Lisa and I went on to complete our next task. We had a hook-up on VIP tickets to the Jill Scott and Maxwell concert that included backstage passes to meet the performers. I knew Tori loved them and would be so surprised because the tickets were sold out as soon as they went on sale. Fortunately, the promoter is one of my dad's best friends.

We had the best seats in the house. It was going to be memorable, to say the least.

Tori

The weekend kept getting better. Lisa's announcement at brunch made me very emotional. It was the icing on the cake for me. I was loving Atlanta, my job, and the prospective relationship with Kenya. Sure, we still had some hurdles to cross but I think we were on the same page.

Last night, I wanted her in the worst way, but she put the brakes on and kept me in check. That, in itself, was a turn on. And that she wanted to take the time to know me, and me, her, was motivation. Yes, sex was still on my mind, but I was willing to wait if it meant we could have a long future together. The way the weekend was playing out, things felt right, but it was still so early.

The concert was exceptional. Jill Scott was sexy. She had such a wide range from soprano to tenor. Maxwell was a crooner. Even though I don't 'do' men, the way he sang, he made me want to do things to him that I haven't done in a long time. All that talent made the Philips Arena seem too small to hold them.

We enjoyed ourselves thoroughly. Meeting them backstage was more than I could have hoped for. Of course I had to snap a few pictures with my 'baby momma' and my 'future baby daddy'. I'm not a celebrity chaser but I sure couldn't wait to catch them in concert again.

We ended the night with a casual sushi dinner. I wasn't fond of sushi but I enjoyed crab cakes and the crab legs. Kenya picked out a nice spot in Atlantic Station that also had a live band. Have you ever been so happy that for no reason at all, you burst into tears? That's how it was for me. I might look a little less than feminine on the outside but I am all woman on the inside. Don't get it twisted.

That night, Kenya and I went to bed as soon as we got in. We were running on fumes. No sleep the night before. Running errands and hanging out all day. It's a wonder we could drive home. We were barely able to walk from the car to the elevator and then to her door. We were that tired. Sex wasn't even on my mind. Lucky for her because after all that good music, I would have tried until I broke her down.

Sunday, late morning, I finally decided to get out of bed. Kenya was already gone and I had no idea what time she left or where she went. I just assumed she and Lisa had more surprises to get in order.

I was trying to convince my body that it was time to get out of bed when Kenya came in. Her racer back tank and running shorts clung to her glistening skin. The strands of hair that managed to get free from her ponytail, blended with the sweat to lay against her face. She was so damn hot! And I'm not talking temperature. Toned legs, muscular thighs, flat abs, and sexy arms. Her ass was like a track star. I couldn't help but ask, "Did you run track?"

"No, I haven't ran competitively. I just run to clear my head and keep in shape. It's more of a stress reliever for me. I run at least three times a week."

"Damn Kenya. You make me feel like a slouch. I haven't worked out since I moved here."

"Maybe we can run together," she said.

"Ummmm, I'm not a runner. I do good just to walk without tripping." She laughed at my admission. "Seriously though, I'm into boxing. I ordered a new punching bag and stand set that should be here any day now. I don't fight competitively, but like with your running, it's a good stress reliever."

"Wow. So that's how you were able to knock out Skye? Impressive."

"Now you know I didn't knock that girl out. Shit. I think my hand took a bigger beating than her face did."

"I know not to piss *you* off."

"You never have to worry about me hitting you. Ever. I'd kill myself before I hurt my woman."

After a brief silence, she responded, "So I'm your woman?"

"Ok, maybe not right now. But I hope I can say that one-day. I am really looking for a lifetime of happiness. I don't want to date frivolously anymore, although the situation with Carmen makes me look like a liar in that regards. I don't know what got into me with her. I think moving here, I was just lonely and as I get closer to thirty, I feel rushed to find that special "one".

"Umm, Tori, in case you forgot, you're already thirty."

As she laughed, I swung a pillow and hit her upside the head. "Hush up. I take that back. Maybe I *will* hit you. With this pillow. Over and over again."

The pillow fight of course turned into a heavy make-out session but again, we managed to summon our will power and stopped it before we lost control and all good sense.

We enjoyed breakfast with the others before planning the rest of our day. Surprisingly, Lisa did not have the day all mapped out. I actually had a say in the agenda.

There was the annual picnic and festival at Piedmont Park. I definitely wanted to check that out. One group had reserved the Georgia Aquarium for the day for a special tour and lunch, but that was in an hour. There was no way we would make that with all of us to get ready.

Kenya showed me a flyer that was emailed to her earlier in the week. A lesbian sorority was staging an open forum discussing today's lesbian relationships. Guests were asked to prepare questions that would then be selected as discussion topics. Since we were all interested, we picked that as our first event. The festival/picnic at the park would be later that afternoon. To end the evening, we elected to attend the Ladies at Play party being held at the French American Brassiere (FAB). A full day of activities mapped out and we were geared up to go.

The forum was held at the gymnasium of Morehouse College. Even though a lesbian, Greek-lettered organization was putting it on, the group encouraged members of other Greek organizations to wear their paraphernalia in demonstration of true pride. Their rationale was if we were truly proud of who we were and whom we chose to love, then we should not be embarrassed to represent our sisterhood organizations while celebrating gay pride.

Our crew was well represented. We each had pledged a member of the Divine Nine, with Dru and I being sorority sisters. We stopped at the Underground and purchased t-shirts and tank tops. At the forum, the vendors had shirts for sale. As well as keychains, novelty license plates, umbrellas, paintings, purses, etc. Of course, we made additional purchases. Kenya joked with the seller about making custom AKA/DST plates like they had for APA/AKA or ZPB/PBS. The seller said she could do it but that Kenya would be causing quite a stir. We were bold, but not *that* bold.

The gym's bleachers were well occupied making it difficult to find seats all together but we managed to find a set of seats in the middle of the audience. Luckily, they had not started or Lisa would have nagged us until we liquored her up. She was a stickler for time.

The discussion leader was a tall, dark woman wearing a pink t-shirt bearing her organization's letters. We had to strain our eyes to see but were able to make out that she was not an AKA.

Kenya speculated, "No, that must be one of the LGBT organizations." There were several of those various groups present as well. It was a really nice turn out for a discussion.

"Welcome to Rainbow Speaks, where we discuss anything from politics to sex to religion. As long as it is pertaining to our lifestyle, all questions are welcome. You should have dropped your questions in the boxes set up at the entrance. If not, worry not; we have a segment at the end where we pick two participants to pose any question they have to the audience. Please give your first name when responding to any of the questions. The only thing we ask is that you are respectful of others. We are all grown women; we need to act as such. There will be no name calling, shouting over another person, or heckling. Security is in full effect so please don't make us have to escort you out. My name is Valerie and I will be your guide as we embark on this month's journey. The theme is PRIDE. Let's begin."

The first question presented was, "Is it acceptable for a stud to be bisexual?" There were definitely mixed feelings on this. One stud said it was a disgrace to other lesbians and studs; especially if that stud dated drag queens or bisexual men. Another countered that as a member of the

LGBT community, we should be able to love who we want to love. Her argument was that we have fought for this freedom and complain when heterosexuals look down their noses at us, so how is it then okay for us to look down on a bisexual whether she dresses feminine or otherwise?

Someone else asked if gay marriage was legalized with all the rights and benefits allowed to heterosexuals, how many of us would get married? I saw Toy squeeze Lisa's hand as Lisa kissed her cheek. Their opinion was evident.

Kenya asked my take on it.

"I would love to walk down the aisle with the woman I love. I am definitely looking for a long-term commitment. Permanent, even. I have no qualms about taking a woman's name or she taking mine. As much money as I pay in taxes, I should be able to marry a cow if I wanted to."

"Girl, you're so stupid," Kenya said, laughing.

Valerie posed the follow-up question, which got the crowd riled up. "After we all run out to get married, how many of us will actually stay together? I mean, look at the rate of divorce among heterosexuals. Can we do better? Our 'rate of turn-over' is pretty high. The average life span of the lesbian relationship is two to five years. Who's to say that marriage would make this any better?"

A chocolate skinned stud stood up to answer. She got several whistles and catcalls. Apparently, she was quite popular. "Hi, I'm Vonda." There was a round of applause.

I turned to Kenya, "Who is she?"

"Oh, she plays for the WNBA team here."

"Ohhhh."

Vonda continued, "Gay relationships don't typically last long. I don't believe being able to legally marry would change that. I feel the divorce rate would be significantly higher." There were grunts of approval and a few that were obvious disagreement.

The next woman who introduced herself as Kizzy said, "I agree with Vonda. Women fight way too much." Her comment was greeted with choruses of "Amen", "Ain't that the truth," and "Preach!" She continued, "But if she asks me, I'm ready!" The audience laughed along with her but gave her a loud round of applause.

Dru stood, "Hi, I'm Dru. I don't know. The way I see it, at the rate straight married couples are going, I think gay couples would do just as well. Hell, maybe even better. But then again, I'm not big on either one so you won't see me running to the courthouse." That got a good laugh out of the women as well.

Another cute stud stood up to speak. "Hey beautiful women. I'm Kelz. If you go back and start converting all the common law marriages, I read somewhere that it doesn't come close to the divorce rate of heterosexual marriage. They stay together longer. Even the cases of domestic violence don't compare. But that's only considering lesbian relationships."

There were some murmurs throughout the crowd. I heard one woman behind us say, "So it's best to live together and not get the benefits that the straight people get? Don't we deserve more than just common law marriages or domestic partnerships?"

A tall stud spoke up. "Kelz, I don't think the number of people in common law marriages accurately represents the number of gays and lesbians in "committed" relationships. However, I do believe that the divorce rate would be significantly lower than that of heterosexual marriages. At least, I'm hoping." She sat, then, remembering the rules, she stood again and said, "Sorry, I'm Mechell."

Kelz stood once again, "Mechell, it kinda does because you can't forget about the couples in their forties, fifties, and sixties who have been together since the 70s and 80s. But today's qualification of common law is only six months in some states, like Texas, and seven years in others, like

Louisiana. If we convert all those, the divorce rate of gays and lesbians would be significantly lower than 'heteros'. Feel me?"

Kelz received a standing ovation for that. It seemed many needed to hear the words, which served as hope for the possibility of a long lasting relationship.

Lisa took her turn. "Hi. I'm Lisa. We can sit here and discuss this all day but it really is based on individual specific factors. Like for me, I am tired of dating and being with a different woman every couple of years. I took the time to find the right one and more time to solidify that she was the right one. Now that I know for sure it's HER, I'm not going anywhere. I know it won't always be easy or fun. Shit, I might want to kill her some times. But all that headache and frustration will be *my* headache and frustration. She'll be *my* strength, *my* backbone, *my* support person. *My* best friend. It's all about how badly you want it to work. People quit too easily. At the first sign of discontent, they run. We're unappreciative and selfish. It's time we made up our minds to fight for the real love that we want. We can do better than heterosexuals because we had to fight harder for what we want. Now, let's fight to keep it together. It's really that simple."

There was such a loud roar of applause and whistles, it made Lisa blush. It was cute. Toy stood up, cheering her the loudest, kissing her passionately for the whole room to see. They were such a sweet couple.

A few more questions and then Valerie announced the date for the next forum session. I saw a lot of cell phones come out. People were making sure to log the date into their phones. Kenya and I followed suit. It would surely be something to check out again. What a great way to put lesbian minds to work. Great thinking leads to amazing progression. And the black lesbian community is a work in progress.

We were walking out of the building when one of Kenya's sorors came running up to greet her. Short with long hair, almond-shaped eyes set in a heart shaped face with strong bone structure, she was a beautiful woman with milk chocolate complexion. She had the prettiest, white smile that stretched from ear to ear it seemed.

"Kenya, I haven't seen you around in a minute," she said while blatantly checking Dru out.

"Hey Mik. I've been busy. These are my friends. That's Toy and Lisa. Tori. And that's Dru." She pointed to each of us as she introduced us, but Mik was focused in on Dru.

Dru took notice, showing mutual attraction. "Hi Mik, nice to meet you. You here by yourself?" she asked her.

Kenya, Lisa, Toy, and I stepped away to let them speak. Knowing Dru, she was already arranging a time for them to see each other again. Proving me right, Dru returned to the group to tell us, "I told her to come out to the LAP party at FAB tonight. She said she might be coming with a few of her friends. Hope yall don't mind."

"Wow, that quick huh?" Kenya asked.

"Dru has a way with women," I answered.

"Watch how you say that, Tori. May make her think I'm some sort of player."

Lisa chimed in, "Heffa, you are! Don't forget, we *know* you. Kenya's just getting to see who you are but we've been around you forever."

We laughed and talked on our way to the festival. We enjoyed seeing so many of the LGBT family out at the park. Kenya knew quite a few people but I guess that's expected since she's lived here all her life. A few of the girls were a bit too friendly though. One girl even pulled her over to the side and tried to run her hand down her back and ass. Toy grabbed my arm before I could make it over there and put the chic in her place. By the way Kenya snatched the girl's arm, I think she did a pretty good job of that on her own, anyway.

Not surprisingly, we ran into Jewelle and Maria. There was no drama though. In fact, they walked right by us as if not seeing us. That was a good thing but still, we were on edge. We spent about two hours at the park then returned to the loft. We needed to relax prior to stepping back out. It was a great day but I was hot, sticky, and ready for a nap.

Hours later we were partying at the FAB with the twenty-five and older crowd. They had three levels of wall-to-wall beautiful women. The music was amazing and the bartenders were earning their tips. One sip of my Absolut Stress and all negative thoughts melted away. The refreshing taste of Absolut, pineapple, orange, and cranberry juices was my signature drink.

Mik and a couple of her friends met up with us on the second floor where the sounds of contemporary and some old school dancehall dominated the Reggae floor. It was fun trying to whine my hips to keep up with Kenya. That girl had a 'dutty whine.' When the DJ switched to rap and hip-hop, she popped her booty as if she had trained at Strokers. I managed to keep up with her though. I think. My friends always said I danced like a white girl.

Mik and Dru seemed to be hitting it off. So much so, that they left us to go up to the rooftop terrace. Lisa became "concerned" when they had been gone for a while. The three of us knew what the deal was. Still, we rode the elevator to the terrace. It was empty.

As we got ready to ride the elevator back down, we heard a stifled moan. Behind the elevator bay, at the darkest corner of the terrace, there was Dru, lip-locked with Mik *and* her hand up her dress. We could only imagine what it was doing there.

I had all intentions of leaving, but peer pressure made me go with Toy, Lisa, and Kenya over to where they were. Toy grabbed her cell phone to snap a picture but we gave ourselves away when Lisa's heel clacked on the concrete deck. Mik yanked her skirt down but all that did was make us laugh louder. Poor thing. She didn't know how we clowned on each other. Fortunately, she eventually joined in the laughter.

I guess Sasha and Dru were officially broken up because Dru had definitely moved on. She deserved better, anyway. She wasn't necessarily a commitment-phobe. She just refused to settle for less. She'd had her share of trifling women. Hate it ended that way for Sasha but didn't we all deserve a chance at love?

14

CHAPTER FOURTEEN

Kenya

We had a great weekend but it was time to get back to work. The girls headed back to Houston to prepare for their upcoming move in September. Tori returned to her condo and we went back to a professional relationship.

At work.

Outside of work we enjoyed quiet dinners at home and an occasional outing. We were still very worried about being caught dating. One of those outings was an open mic night in midtown. Tori kept talking about how she was missing the open mic event she went to regularly in Houston.

"It's called HeArt & Soul. A friend invited me out but I was hesitant because I was never really a fan of open mic before. It seemed the people were pretentious and tried to fool people into thinking they were deeper than they actually were," she said. "But when I went to HeArt & Soul, even the environment was different. It was a lighthearted, joyful place. I felt welcomed. There were spoken word artists, of course, but there were other talented artists displaying their craft as well. Visual artists, graphic designers, singers, musicians, jewelry makers, authors. You name it, they had it. Even if when you left your house you had no talent, by the time you got there, you felt inspired. Whether it be to write, take up photography, give back to your community, or just better yourself. And it was so entertaining. I don't think I ever left there without laughing. The creator and host, K. Dapree, he did an awesome job in developing it. When I first started going, it was in a small building but they grew by leaps and bounds and now they pack the place in a much larger venue. I'm telling you, Kenya, you've never seen an open mic event of this size."

So of course, I had to show her what the A-T-L had to offer. She liked the little spot and I think she enjoyed most of it but she still insisted it couldn't compare to her beloved HeArt & Soul.

The small café was filled with patrons. A four-piece band played jazz music while the performers and audience used the tunes to get into the mood. The scent of freshly brewed coffee tickled my nose. I loved roasted coffee beans.

The spoken word artists took their turn on the stage, letting their words disturb, stimulate, and even make love to our minds. A young lady, classy and sophisticated with diction to be envious of, got on the mic.

"Good evening. My name is Ruby Dee. I hope you appreciate this piece. It is near and dear to me."

Depths

I want to go with you to the depths of the earth
I want to go with you to the end of the ocean and see the sun gleam in your eyes
I want to take you…everywhere without even taking one step and show you the glory of the magnitude of my heart
Will you go with me?

No, of course not….
Why? Because every step you took before me weighed nine hundred ninety nine pounds and would have been one thousand but she thought she was doing you a favor by carrying that last one…
She drenched your soul with cruel words while hammering away at your spirit with the anchor of her baggage
Need I even continue?

I want to show you the world…
Give you the passion I know you need….
Can I come in?
Can you open your heart without me opening my legs so that I can see the real you?
See what lies beneath the tragedy and hurt and the sorrow and pain…
Show you that love doesn't need a bandage…and doesn't impose shame…
Let me show you my world

A world laced in Chantilly and outlined in gold…

Paths with so many highlights of color you won't need a rainbow...
It's me...
It's me you see who can take you there...
Why won't you just go with me?

I feel like I'm walking this road alone...
With no one in sight...
With no one to share my insights...
I'm alone...
Alone...I say...
I converse alone..I travel alone.... I shop alone...
I work alone...I read alone...I cook alone...
I go out alone...I drive alone...I lay alone...
I pray alone... I love alone...But why?
 Weren't you just here with me?
Didn't we just share this moment...this time...
This place...where did you just go?

Are you so far removed that you feel you can't connect or are you so
far disconnected you have removed yourself from the situation at
hand...

And if you can answer either way...Today is not your day but a new
day because I'm moving on...

Because there has to be someone else who wants to take me to the
depths of the earth
And there has to be someone who wants to take me to the end of the
ocean and see the sun gleam in my eyes
Someone who wants to take me everywhere without taking me
anywhere at all because all I need is right there at home...

I just might go with her...
Why? Because when you have someone who carries your
burdens...your steps don't weigh nearly as much...
She drenches my soul with passion and fire and heat and desire...She
takes me above the world...everyday...

She's there with me even when she's not there and never EVER makes
me feel alone...
We talk together.....and walk together...and shop together...
And read together...and cook together...and travel together....

And pray together…and lay together…and make love together…

She and I are one…
And when she met me, she told me I was THE one…
Shit, I guess Jay was right…
Lose one…Let go to get one….
You were just one but you just lost one…

----Brittny "Ruby Dee" Mandarino

When I tell you that piece so fit with my current situation. Have you ever read a book that seemed to be written about your life? Almost like it was your autobiography? That's how I felt about Ruby Dee's poetry. She always stirred emotions within me. Sometimes pleasant, other times, not so much.

Tori went crazy over one particular spoken word artist who went by the name Ntense. She got up on the mic and spit words that made you squirm in your seat. One in particular went like this:

Without a Strap
I fucked her without a strap.
Yet, I penetrated her with my pussy
And my eyes.
Thrusting her hips against my hips,
Her wetness spread from her toes,
To my fingertips…
I could taste her pleasure…

I fucked her without a strap.
Yet, I touched spots an
8 inch "cock" couldn't rock...
Instead, my fingers ran deep,
And her white 'dialect'
Had an ironic twist of a French accent
If heard with virgin ears...
But still...her words made sense to me.
I fucked her without a strap.
Yet, my caress was simply explicit
In ways to illicit
A side of me that's been hidden.
She fucked ME without a strap.
Yet, her words
Flowed across my skin
Like coffee touching my lips,
The back of my throat
With each sip,
My thoughts,
My body,
Would dip deeper and deeper and deeper into her.
But when I DID fuck her with a strap,
She arched her back
And well...
That's a different story.

When she finished the piece, the audience went wild with applause. And little, raunchy, Miss Tori just *had* to go shake her hand, and even bought a copy of her book of poetry. Then, she read that poem to me about three times before we made it home. I didn't care. I enjoyed spending time with her.

We spent July 4th with my parents at their home. My mother invited all our relatives and friends to the "small barbecue." My parents didn't know how to do anything small. There were at least one hundred people spread between the house, the backyard and pool, and the guesthouse that contained the game and media rooms.

All those people around meant Tori and I were forced to appear as just friends. Although I was out to my parents and some family members, there were those relatives that you didn't want in you business at all. They'd take a simple story and spin it to make a soap opera or something off of Judge Judy.

At least Tori was able to meet my mother, who fell in love with her on first appearance. Tori had decided to wear jeans and a fitted t-shirt. She didn't look like a stud, but she didn't try to fake it by being all girlie. I ended up wearing jeans and a tank top.

It was hot that day so we wore our bathing suits under our clothes with hopes of taking a quick dip once most of the people left. Instead, we jumped right into the pool once the first few people got in. There were no public displays of affection, although we snuck a few touches in the pool, underwater. We played a few games of pool with some of my relatives and poker with some of the fellas. We ate so much food I thought I would bust.

Because we were both on call that night, we left before the fireworks but not before my parents extended an open invitation for Tori to join us again for dinner sometime. She made quite an impression on my parents. They'd not been receptive to any of the other women I brought around, still hoping I would "grow out of it" and marry a man. Today, they seemed to finally accept my lifestyle. Maybe it took me bringing the right woman around.

On call at AGH was very busy. Of course, I'd been on call for surgery before but being on call with anesthesia was very different. Although I wasn't actually doing any anesthesia, Tori allowed me to place breathing tubes and IVs as well as write post-operative pain control orders. Being Fourth of July night, there were quite a few trauma surgeries which meant lots of experience under my belt. It's amazing how people can drink, do drugs, smoke weed, and then try to drive.

The rest of summer flew by. Our patient numbers were up significantly from last year and with word of mouth from current patients, the pain service expanded to accommodate the new patient growth.

Tori was named head of that service when Dr. Sanchez went on disability. His morbid obesity led to deterioration of his knee joints. Hence, not only did Tori have to hire new anesthesia providers but she also had to replace Dr. Sanchez with an experienced pain relief provider.

She tried feebly to convince me to change my specialty but she knew as well as I, that I was looking forward to being done with training. There was no way in hell I planned on going back for more. Not even for her. She said she had to try but understood where I was coming from.

She spent a good bit of time, outside of work, interviewing candidates. She loved her job but I know it was more than she'd expected. I tried to help out as much as I could at work and at home. I kept her refrigerator stocked with food from my mom's Sunday dinners, washed her clothes when I washed mine, and let my cleaning lady clean her place whenever she came to clean mine.

To add more stress to her, someone slashed all her tires while her car was parked in the garage at work. The security department said the cameras were nonfunctional at the time so we were unable to say for sure who did it. We had a list of suspects. Jewelle, Carmen, or Skye. Anyone of them was capable. And certainly pissed enough to do it.

When she replaced the tires, someone wrote BITCH in lipstick all over her windshield. She tried to act as if it were no big deal, but I could see it was all taking a toll on her. She didn't smile nearly as much and except at work or when we went to church, I didn't get to spend much time with her. She was forever trying to catch up on sleep and she lost a few pounds.

As Labor Day weekend approached, I was looking forward to a quiet relaxing weekend with her. It was also Black Pride weekend so I thought we would also party a little.

Lisa, Toy, and Dru were back and moving into their new home but when we tried to contact Tori to assist with the move, we were unable to reach her.

We called and left several messages for her at work and her cell phone. No one at the hospital had seen her since Thursday evening. When I left my place to go help Lisa, I saw her car was still parked in her space. I immediately ran back upstairs and knocked on her door. When she didn't answer, I used the key she gave me a few weeks earlier, to gain access.

Once inside, I found her bedroom door was locked. I knocked but there was no response. I tried to use the metal key hole probe to unlock the door but my hands were shaking too badly. I finally gave up and after a few tries, kicked the door in.

There she was resting peacefully in bed. Or so it appeared. I shook her and called her name. She didn't stir. I checked to see if she were breathing. She was. I palpated her pulse. It was weak and thready, but it was present. I called 911 and then called Lisa. When EMS came, they placed her on a stretcher but even then, she didn't move. Her limp body was covered with a blanket, as she was loaded into the ambulance.

Lisa, Dru, and Toy met us at the emergency room. Tori was diagnosed with viral meningitis and encephalitis and admitted to the ICU after several tests and an MRI.

Lisa called Tori's mother and father who took the next flight to Atlanta. It was good to meet her parents but not under those circumstances. Her mom broke into tears when she saw her only daughter hooked to a host of tubes and wires. Her father's face was also full of distraught.

"Tori has always been so strong," her mother said as she held her hand. "She's worked so hard to get here and now my poor baby . . ." she ended as sobs racked through her body.

The medical team placed a few IVs for antibiotics, pain medicines, and IV fluids. She was breathing on her own though, not requiring a breathing tube. Instead, she had a face mask with oxygen.

She had spiked a fever on the way to the hospital so they were thinking she had become sick overnight. Judging by her range of symptoms, they were estimating she got infected within the last 48 hours. Her recent state of exhaustion decreased the strength of her immune system. We performed a record number of epidural pain blocks within the last couple of weeks so she probably was exposed to an infected patient and contracted the virus that then spread to her spinal fluid and circulated around her brain.

The MRI results from earlier that morning showed minimal involvement of the important intracranial structures so a full recovery was expected. It was just a matter of time. Even knowing this, it was still very difficult to see her like that.

The other anesthesia providers in her group came to visit sporadically. All day Friday, she had a steady stream of visitors but she wouldn't know it. She was still unconscious.

The ICU rules allowed two visitors at a time but because she was a hospital employee, they made an exception to the rule for her family, Lisa, and I. Some of her coworkers who knew me as her trainee gave me questioning looks but no one actually said anything.

By Friday night, we decided I would take Tori's parents to her place to rest up overnight and Lisa and I would stay at her bedside. In the morning, they would drive her car back up here and sit with her while Lisa and I rested.

On the drive to the loft, not much was said. Her mom wasn't crying as much, but she was still very shaken up. They hadn't seen Tori's place before so I gave them a quick tour and showed them how to access the parking garage.

Since Tori's room was probably infected, I set them up in the guest bedroom. I called my cleaning lady to clean and disinfect her room and the common areas. My mom had dropped some food off at the hospital once she heard that Tori's parents were in town, but they said they were too tired to eat so I put all the food in the refrigerator before I went back to the hospital.

Lisa and I slept in two recliners in the far corner of her room. They didn't want us too close to Tori since she was considered infectious. They'd already drawn my blood to see if I contracted the virus since I worked closely with her. The tests were negative. I hadn't contracted the virus.

The nurses came in and out throughout the night to check on her. At around 4:00 am, the vital signs monitor began alarming, waking us with a start. The nurses, doctors, and respiratory therapists rushed in and within seconds, the room was in chaos. Tori's temperature was in the danger zone and she began having febrile seizures. I watched her body shake violently. My heart beat out of my chest.

I have seen so many seizures in action. I should not have been fazed by it. But when the person you love is having the seizure, it's the scariest thing in the world. Lisa and I huddled in the far corner, allowing the team space to work. We prayed together silently as they barked and carried out orders. During the seizure, Tori stopped breathing so they ended up placing a breathing tube. Now she really looked bad. Once she was stabilized, Lisa called Tori's parents, Dru, and Toy.

I called my parents to keep them abreast of the situation. My father, hearing the news, rushed to the hospital. He took over her care, ordering medications to prevent further convulsions and a hypothermia protocol to decrease her core temperature. He was hoping that would decrease her risk of having another seizure.

It was late Tuesday afternoon before Tori's temperature returned to normal. When it was sure she was out of the woods, her status was downgraded from critical to serious. The breathing tube was removed and my father discontinued the seizure medications.

During the time she was on the ventilator, I stayed at the hospital, running to shower in my father's call room and using hospital scrubs. When her parents were visiting, I stayed in the call room to sleep, not wanting to be too far away. But once they returned to the loft, I went back to her bedside to sit and pray.

On that Tuesday when they declared her stable, her parents stayed at the hospital while I ran home to take a quick shower. I cried the whole way home and in the shower. I put cold packs on my eyes to relieve the puffiness before going back to the hospital. If everybody else was going to be crying, I wanted to be strong.

That night, as Tori's parents were preparing to return to her condo, Tori shifted in the bed. A few minutes later, she opened her eyes and tried to sit up. I notified the nurses who in turn contacted my father in his call room down the hall. Apparently my mom had been staying there with him because she rushed in with him as well.

Once they verified she was fully conscious, they removed her oxygen mask and changed her records to reflect her stable condition. She was showered with hugs, even though they told us she was still under isolation precautions. She was so surprised to see everyone there, especially her parents.

"What are you guys doing here? How long was I asleep?" she asked.

"We're guessing since Thursday night," her mother replied. "You scared us, baby. Your father and I jumped on a plane right away. You know how he's scared to fly."

"Sheila, stop lying to that girl," he said in his deep voice. "She knows you're the one scared of flying."

With Tori awake and being attended to by her parents and Lisa, I felt like I faded into the background. Though dejected and disappointed, I understood that family came first, so I tried to slip quietly out the door.

Tori's weak voice called out, "Where do you think you're going, woman? You're the reason I got all these people in my room. Don't try to escape now." Even as sick as she was, she still maintained her sense of humor. I went to meet her outstretched hand. She took hold of my hand and with what strength she could muster she gave it a squeeze.

"Thank you for being here with me this whole time. And thank you for finding me. My mom said you kicked in my bedroom door. I knew you were feisty," she teased.

As silent tears flowed faster than I could wipe then away, I said, "You're welcome. Please don't scare me like that again."

We spent the rest of the night filling her in on the excitement she caused. Her parents went back to her place to sleep and Lisa, Dru, and Toy, went home. I refused to leave her side. My father offered me his on call room but I opted to stay in the room with her, so as an alternative solution, he had us moved to a large suite on the floor. She was stable enough not to require ICU any longer.

I slept with her in the hospital bed that night. It was the first time we had slept in the same bed since the weekend of her birthday. So much had changed since then. Including my fear of our relationship being found out. After almost losing her, I was willing to take the risk. Anything, for the chance at love.

15

CHAPTER FIFTEEN

Tori

If it weren't for the fact that I was actually lying in the hospital bed with tubes and wires coming from every part of my body, I would not have believed what they said I went through. I was feeling extremely tired when I went to bed that Thursday night but just chalked it up to me working extra hard to get the practice to where it needed to be. I didn't have so much as a sniffle, so how on earth did I get that sick? And a breathing tube? Really? That was a bit much. I've never had the flu and here I go with meningitis and encephalitis. What can I say? When I do it, I do it big!

On Sunday morning, I laid wide-awake with Kenya curled up at my side. She was so tired. I couldn't believe she stayed with me that whole time. And to think I doubted whether she was worth the risk of getting caught and penalized by the hospital.

Sure, I loved my job. Had worked hard to get to where I am now but at some point, one had to ask what was more important. A lifetime of happiness, love, and family, or a job position. Because that's all it was. I had no doubt I could find another position right here in Atlanta. It might not have the same perks but that was not reason enough to give up on a chance at love.

I still wanted us to take our time though. I strongly believe that for love to last, it needed to crescendo. No jumping from start to finish. It needed to develop, like a good orgasm. We all know the best orgasms are the ones that start soft and slow but then gradually build up to the point where you can't take it anymore. Then it explodes into colorful fireworks. That's how I needed this to be.

Next to me, Kenya stirred. I closed my eyes, pretending to be asleep and tried to slow my breathing to a slow rate. I felt her shift to her elbow to better look at me. Her hand caressed my face and her soft lips kissed my cheek. She sighed deeply before getting out of bed. Before she was fully on her feet, I grabbed her hand, pulling her down to me, her body splayed across mine. It was then I realized I had seen her face before.

Okay, I know you are thinking, *Duh, of course you've seen her face. You've been dating her for the last three months.* But that wasn't it. It was in that dream I had my first night in Atlanta. Before I even met her. The sun shone across her facial planes as it did that morning. Her eyes sparkled, even in her current state of exhaustion. She smiled at me and I knew. It was HER. She was "the one" I'd been hoping for.

Her smiling expression morphed into one of concern. "Are you okay? You need me to call my father or the nurse?" she asked with apprehension etched into her face.

"No. No, I'm good. Just lay with me."

"Okay but if you're feeling sick again, please tell me. I don't want to have to go through again what we just experienced. It was hard seeing you like that. I was so scared I was going to lose you."

"Aaaaawww, poo poo, you were worried about me." I teased.

She hit me on my thigh just hard enough to hurt but not enough to bruise. "Ouch! What's that for?" I asked.

"Don't patronize me Tori. You know we were beyond worried."

"*We*, huh? How about you tell me how *you* felt." You can call it having my ego stroked, but I needed to hear her say it. I needed to hear it for myself even though I saw it in her eyes.

"Tori, I was scared shitless. You'd been working so hard and I was mad that you couldn't make time for me. It was selfish, I know, but it's the truth. I missed you. And then when you got sick, my heart threatened to shatter in my chest. Seeing you in that ICU bed with IVs, monitors, an oxygen mask --- it was too much for me, I'm strong, but the thought of losing you broke me down. I love you. I know it's only been a short while but I really do. I love you."

It's what I needed to hear. I wanted to kiss her right then but since I was still on isolation, I would risk making her sick and that just wasn't an option. Instead, I said, "I love you too, Kenya. And yes, it's only been a few months, but I won't put love on a time scale. It is what it is. C'est la vie. As long as you love me too, that's proof enough that it's the right time for *us*."

She leaned in to kiss me on the lips but I turned my head to give her my cheek. "I don't want you to get sick. If you were to get as sick as I did, I would surely lose my mind."

"As crazy as that sounded, that's really romantic," she crooned. "Dr. Smith came by on Friday. He said you've been placed on sick leave. You have to be off for two weeks per my dad's orders. Strict bed rest. And then Dr. Smith wants you to take an extra week off on top of that. He said your patients have been rescheduled. I happen to have four weeks vacation time saved up. Maybe we can go somewhere."

"A vacation already? I just started working. I don't know."

"Tori, you really don't have much of a say in it. You'll be in violation of the hospital's infection control policy. You have to be at home for a minimum of two weeks after you've been fever free for forty-eight hours. You had a fever yesterday, so if you went home tomorrow, that's mid-September before you can go back to work. And then your chief said he doesn't want to see you until a week after that. That's end of September, early October."

"Wow," I said in resignation, "I guess I have no choice. A forced vacation. That's a first. Okay. Let me call Lisa to see if they want to tag along. We maybe can do that little resort on Jamaica that we've been checking out since last year."

"It's booked solid. Lisa and I talked about it last night before she left. There's a nice rental house on the beach though, not too far from that resort. It's being arranged as we speak."

"Well in that case, how about you continue working, don't use up all your vacation time for me. You can just take that last week off and the five of us will go traveling."

"Make that the six of us. Dru's bringing company."

"Ah fuck no she ain't! I can't be around Sasha's crazy ass. Especially not for a whole week." It was bad enough Dru dissed me and went back to that girl, but her ass was crazy. She hated that we were still friends. It'd be just my luck she killed me in my sleep.

"No. Remember they broke up. Calm down."

"That's never stopped them from getting back together before."

"Well this time it's different. She's been seeing Mik since June. Mik has even been to Houston a few times."

This was news to me. I guess you miss a lot when you are too busy to talk to you're friends. I'd have to make an extra effort to catch up on everyone's life. "Okay, well I'm glad to hear. What else did Lisa come up with? I know she has it all planned out already." Jamaica for a week, and then back to Atlanta. I was excited just thinking about it. Kenya and I hadn't been sexually intimate as yet but that could make for a very romantic and memorable first time.

Lisa must have heard us talking about her because she showed up shortly thereafter. She gave me the tightest hug. "You look so much better Tori. You had them scared. Poor Kenya cried nonstop."

"Now wait a minute Lisa," Kenya responded, "You were crying more than anybody. Even her momma."

"Don't go acting all spunky now that your girl's back from the brink of death." They laughed. I just shook my head.

16

CHAPTER SIXTEEN

Tori

That following Sunday, after being in the hospital for over a week, Tori was finally discharged home. Between her parents, Lisa, Toy, and Dru, she had more than enough people to help out while I went to work. My schedule was pretty light since all the patients had to be rescheduled until Tori could return to work. By then, my rotation with the pain service would be over and I'd be back to working in the operating room. I loved being around Tori but I was so ready to go back to what I loved most. Surgery.

With all her friends and family there, the time I was able to spend with Tori was limited. With all her visitors, we had very little privacy. When we did get alone time, she talked about work. Excessively. The girl was a workaholic. I loved my job too, but obviously not nearly as much as she did since she couldn't seem to shut up about it.

I mentioned this to Lisa just to get another perspective. She told me to be patient and assured me Tori was only like this when she was away from work for long periods. It was her way of staying on her game when she couldn't physically be in the game.

So I sucked it up for two weeks. Listening to her findings from all the research journals she read throughout the day. She even managed to conduct several phone interviews and hired three more anesthesia providers to lighten her load. That was a bright spot for me because that meant we would have more time to spend with one another when she did return to work.

On that Friday, two weeks after Tori had been rushed to the emergency room, I left the hospital at around 2:30 pm, to find all the windows in my car had been busted in. Again, the security guard on duty claimed not to have seen or heard anything and the camera, although functioning that day, had decided not to capture any video during the time frame when it could have occurred. How fucking convenient! *When I get back from Jamaica, I am going to find Carmen and kick her ass.* I had no doubt it was Carmen. She was evil and vindictive. But she was messing with the wrong one.

After the hospital police left, I found a typed note in the armrest console of my car, where I kept my sunglasses. It read, *"You've pissed me off. Now prepare to have your whole life ruined."* That shook me to the core. Could Carmen be that evil? *Yes.* I should have taken the note to the police but instead I drove straight to the dealership to have the windows replaced and the broken glass vacuumed out. Although I was shaken by the incident, I didn't want Tori to know about it and get worried. That would surely make her sick again and we didn't need that. I would tell her once we got back from a nice relaxing vacation.

Luckily, the dealership had my windows in stock. Unfortunately, it would be Monday before they could be installed. They issued me a loaner vehicle and I drove home. When asked, I would just tell Tori I took my car in for a detailing. There was nothing else I could do about it between now and the trip. Just one other thing to handle when I get back.

I arrived home that evening to two less visitors. Tori's parents flew out earlier in the day. The girls were camped out on Tori's couch when I got in. Tori looked so much better. Her color had returned and her eyes were bright again. Her body still looked a little slim but not nearly as frail as when she was in the hospital. Her hair was freshly styled.

"Cute," I told her. "I really like it. You should wear it like that more often."

"Thanks babe. Had to cut off about two inches though. Having it loose like that when I was sick, really broke it off in some areas. She had to do a deep treatment. You know it's just gonna crinkle back up once we get in the water."

"Don't forget to tell her about our spa day," Lisa prompted her.

"You went to the spa? How was it?" I asked.

"It was amazing! Lisa kept *bugging* me about it," she said pointedly, "but I'm glad she finally dragged me out the house to do it. I'm not only recuperated, I feel better than before." As she spoke, her eyes got brighter, her cheeks more flushed, and her happiness radiated through her dimpled smile.

I wanted her to stay like that forever. Telling her about the vandalism to my car would surely ruin her mood. If I told her about the note, she'd be stressed beyond what she was before she took ill. There was no way I was going to put all that on her.

"Kenya, Kenya!" The worried pitch of Tori's voice

broke me out of my reverie. "You haven't been listening to me. Are you ok?"

"Oh yea. I'm fine. Just tired I guess. Took the car to get detailed. They'll keep it for me until we get back. I have to pack. Did you guys get swimsuits?"

Dru answered. "These femmes --- Yes, you too, Tori cause you done turned all girlie on us --- these chics had us all over Lenox mall looking for bathing suits. Think they each have ten. Shit! I hate shopping with femmes."

"Shut up, Dru!" yelled Lisa.

"Whatever, it's the truth. Am I lying, dog?" she looked to Toy for support. Lisa gave Toy a warning glare but Toy answered anyway.

"Naw, you ain't telling nothing but the truth. I'm so glad we're moving here so the 'fish' can go shopping together and leave us be."

"You know what? I'ma 'leave you be' alright," said Lisa, annoyed. "Don't expect NONE on this here trip. You can go snuggle with Dru. How about that?" Lisa went into the bedroom and slammed the door. We all laughed.

Toy yelled to her, "I just might do that."

Just as quickly as Lisa walked out the room, she marched back into the room, smacking Toy on the back of the head and hurling couch pillows at Dru and Tori. That just made them laugh that much louder.

They were still laughing and playing around when the house phone rang. Tori answered it but couldn't hear above the noise so she took the phone into her room. I took the opportunity to escape to my condo to pack and straighten up a bit. I also needed time to figure things out. Somebody -- likely Carmen -- was out to get us and I needed to stop it before things went too far.

Tori

When I saw the UNKNOWN flash across the caller ID, I assumed it was Mik calling for directions. Instead, the unfamiliar voice issued a threat.

"You fucked with me. Now, you're fucked. I would tell you to watch your back but I'm watching it for you. I'm watching every move you make, bitch." Then she hung up.

I told Lisa, Dru, and Toy about the call but asked them not to mention it to Kenya. I didn't want her to worry. I'd brought her enough stress with my hospitalization. They agreed to keep things quiet but encouraged me to tell Kenya after the trip.

"I'll think about it," I told them.

Shortly after, Mik arrived and we all went out to eat. I

enjoyed spending time with all the girls but there was a gnawing feeling in the back of my mind. I really did feel like I was being watched, but we made it through dinner without incident.

CHAPTER SEVENTEEN

Tori

It was a smooth plane ride from Atlanta to Jamaica.
We moved quickly to collect our bags from baggage claim
before hailing a taxi to take us to the villa at Rainbow
Beach on the south side of the island. That ride wasn't so
smooth. I think we hit every pothole ever created. My ass
felt like it was being beat with a paddle. I couldn't wait to
get to our destination.

I tried to appreciate the bright orange, red, fuchsia,
pink, and purple bougainvilleas as we drove through the
villages. The two and three story concrete wall homes sat
on the sides of hills, some low in the valley, and others
scattered along the roadside. Goats and cows took up
residence in nearby pastures, lending their scents to the
wind. Lisa closed all the windows in the eight-seater van to

help eliminate the scent, but the nonfunctioning A/C quickly changed her mind. Being able to breathe was more important that what scent we breathed.

Luckily, the driver hauled ass, delivering us to the villa in one piece but in just forty-five minutes. The brochure stated the beach was an hour and a half from the airport. I'd say we made pretty good time.

The driver dropped us off at the one-story, turquoise blue beach house. The concrete house was sprawling and just steps from the beach. It was surrounded by towering coconut, tamarind, and mango trees. Plump, juicy mangoes hung from the lower branches. Mangoes were definitely going to be on the menu in some sort or fashion. I *loved* mangoes.

The six of us stood in awe of our surroundings. There were some of the same colorful bougainvillea bushes scattered around the property. Oleander bushes flanked the foundation of the house. There was a grassy area followed by fine white sand, which led to blue waters that shone like glass. The water was calm today with just an occasional silent wave. Sea gulls sang as they flew from tree to tree before diving to catch their lunch.

"This is beautiful," Kenya said breathily. I took hold of her hand pulling her closer to me. It was a moment to share with someone special and there was no one else I would have wanted to spend it with.

Toy and Lisa hurried ahead to the entrance. The key was under mat just as the owner had promised. As we entered the foyer, we all squealed and oooohed and aaaahed with excitement. There was the largest open living room we had ever seen with what had to be the world's largest sectional. It faced a large, wall-mounted TV and the room itself was bright from the light coming from the floor to ceiling windows. There was a direct view of the beach and a small island or sand dune about fifty feet from the shoreline. Palm trees framed the window and continued up and down the beach.

The couch was made of bright, neon-patterned fabric, coordinating with the shag rug, contemporary tables, and the dining furniture. The living room opened up to a large kitchen with a lunch spread obviously freshly prepared based on the smells floating around the room. Steam rose from the pots and pans neatly arranged on the industrial cook top. The growling of our stomachs was heard over our chatter reminding us we hadn't eaten since way before sunset that morning.

After a quick washing of hands and grace, we started inspecting the pots and pans. Mik and Lisa grabbed plates while the rest of us spread the food out on the kitchen island, buffet style. Baked fish, conch, shrimp, crabmeat, white rice, boiled green bananas, and fried dumplings were on the menu. If anyone of us was allergic to seafood, we would so have been screwed. Fortunately, that was not the case as we devoured the spread with some of the local sodas to wash it all down.

"That shit was so good," Dru said through a full mouth of food.

"Hell yea!" Toy co-signed.

The rest of us were too full to comment but our opinion was evident as we slumped in our chairs, unbuckling pants, undoing buttons, and patting fat stomachs.

After we cleaned up, we set off to explore the rest of the house. There were four bedrooms, each with their own bathroom, and each on separate corners of the house. The rooms seemed identical except for the colors. Lisa and Toy took the blue room. The bedspread and furniture were covered in blue printed fabric. The bathroom walls were covered in variations of blue glass mosaic tile.

Dru and Mik moved into the orange room and Kenya and I chose the yellow room. Kenya wanted the pink room but that wasn't flying with me. Each bathroom had a two-person tub and separate shower with body sprayers and dual showerheads. Saying it was luxurious would be an understatement. Large bladed ceiling fans hung from the ceiling, circulating the fresh ocean breeze through the room. Soft music played on the central radio system/intercom.

After placing our luggage in our respective rooms, we continued touring the property. Right off the living room there was a patio with a small lap pool and on the farthest corner, a hot tub. There was also an outdoor shower. The beach was just a stone's throw away and as we walked the distance, our feet sank into the warm sand.

"This is better than the spa," I said as a soft wind whipped my hair and the scent of the salt water wafted around me. We dipped our toes into the water, surprised to find it warm.

"Let's go in," Dru suggested.

"No, babe," Mik answered before Lisa's smart remark could roll off her tongue. Mik was a fast learner. "You could catch a cramp."

"And since your ass can't swim, you better not, cause ain't nobody dragging your ass out the water" Lisa still managed to slip in.

"Don't be like that Lisa. Toy can't swim either." Mik

defended.

"True, but you don't hear her talking about going in the water."

"That's cause she already said she doesn't plan on going in at all."

"Why yall bringing me into this? I'm minding my own business," Toy called out from the edge of the water. "Since we're not going into the water now, I think I'ma take a nap. That food gave me the '-itis.' You know how I get after I eat."

We had to agree. I think we were all jet lagged so a nap sounded really good. We walked back to the house and to our individual rooms with the plan being to get up in two hours for a swim. However, that nap turned into sleeping. Kenya was the first one up. At six a.m.!

"Tori!" she called as she shook me. "Wake up."

Rubbing my eyes, I tried to remember where I was. It came back to me slowly. "What time is it?" I asked.

"Six o'clock."

"We took a long nap. I'm hungry. What's for dinner?"

"It's six o'clock in the morning, Tori."

I sat straight up. "You've got to be kidding me. I thought the sun was setting."

"Nope. That's sunrise. We wasted a whole day here."

Then came the knock on our door. "Wake up fools!" Dru called from the other side. Kenya padded over to the door, opening it for Dru and Mik to come in. "Man, we must have been really tired to sleep through the night like that. We didn't even wake up to eat."

"It's the jet lag, sea breeze, and full bellies." Lisa came in practically dragging Toy with her. "We got up around midnight but I think everybody was knocked out. We thought we heard a knocking at the door but nobody was there when we checked."

"Maybe we should call the owner today to see if he came by," Kenya said. "Although I can't see why he would come so late. Maybe he thought we would be up partying, like we should have been. We have seven days here and we've already wasted one."

We grunted but it was the truth. Toy finally spoke, "What are we going to do today?"

We tossed around ideas and made a list of all the things we wanted to do on our vacation. Snorkeling, kayaking, jet skis, Dunn's River Falls, rafting on the Martha Brae, and of course, partying. We also wanted to visit some of the islands popular attractions. Lisa, taking control as usual, came up the idea that we each should pick one attraction to see and one activity that we wanted to do for each day of the trip.

Since this trip was all because of me, I got to pick first. I had heard so much about Dunn's River Falls; I certainly had to check it out. And for the afternoon and evening, I wanted to have a bonfire on the little sand dune or mini island thing sitting out in the water. Toy and Dru didn't seem too excited about the idea, mainly because they were afraid to get that far into the water, but Kenya assured them the water was only waist deep.

"We can even give yall's scary asses some life vests," clowned Lisa.

"Shut up, Lis!" replied Dru. "We just want to make sure, that's all."

"No. Yall are scared. I'm going to make sure you two learn to swim before we leave here. Even if I have to drag you far out into the water and leave you there."

"The hell you are!" responded Toy.

We let them bicker back and forth, enjoying the entertainment.

After an early morning walk on the beach, we had breakfast and made arrangements to be picked up by the driver we used the day before. He drove wild. His van didn't have working A/C. But the man was cheap and fast. We were at the Falls by ten a.m.

(Kenya)

Dunn's River Falls is a popular tourist attraction near Ochos Rios. The waterfall area was surrounded by lush vegetation, the scent of salt water from the nearby ocean, and the call of birds. We arrived mid morning which the tour guide said was a perfect time because the tourist rush had not begun.

We gave the tour guide, Sam, our cameras and camcorders to capture the experience. He trekked ahead of us giving a spiel about the history of the falls and the number of visitors they had each year. I tuned that portion out because out of the corner of my eye, I thought I saw Carmen.

I excused myself from the group with the excuse of having to run to the restroom before we made it to the actual falls. Tori raised an eyebrow but didn't verbalize.

I took the path to the restroom that I thought I saw Carmen going into. Opening the door, I bumped into her. The expression on her face said she was surprised to see me. Or maybe just surprised that *I* saw *her*. She'd made some changes to herself. Something about her seemed happier. Brighter. Her curly fro had grown out since I had last seen her and she was now wearing it straight. She'd gained a little weight but toned up as well as if she'd been working out regularly. I hated to say it but she looked pretty good.

"Are you following us?" she asked.

"Us, who? And why in the hell would I want to follow *you*?"

She was wise to take a few steps back. I *was* tempted to hit her again.

"I'm here with a few friends visiting my family," she said.

"I'm here with a few friends too but I'm sure you know that."

She feigned a confused look. "How would I know that?" she asked.

"Look chick, don't play dumb. You fucked up my car!" I yelled. She backed up to the stall, fearing my next move.

"I don't know what you're talking about. I've been here for the last two weeks. Before that I was busy moving. I swear, I haven't been anywhere near the hospital."

"I didn't say it happened at the hospital. How did you know that?"

Quick on her feet, she replied, "Had to be the hospital. Your condo garage is secured."

"Bullshit! So is the hospital's garage but if you know somebody in security. . ." And that's when it hit me. Jewelle had gotten into the hospital's parking garage without an access card that first day she came to see me. She must know someone in security and got him or her to disable the cameras and let her in.

Fuck! Jewelle was the one trashing our cars and threatening me. Surely she couldn't be that pissed that I chose Tori over her. It wasn't even that serious between us. Damn lesbians and their overly emotional shit.

Yet and still, the realization made my stomach do flip-flops. I stepped back to lean against the wall. I needed to speak to Jewelle as soon as possible. Talk some sense into her. She may not be able to cause us physical harm, herself, but she had the resources to have someone else do it. I needed to reason with her.

Carmen stayed quiet as I let this new idea ramble through my mind. Through the silence, I heard Tori and Lisa's voice approaching so I quickly shoved Carmen into the nearest stall and told her, "Keep quiet." Then I turned to the sink, pretending to wash my hands.

"We were beginning to think you fell in," Lisa joked.

"Oh, I'm fine. Just had to pee before we got into the water. Yall can go ahead. I think I have to go again. Must be all that coconut water we drank this morning."

"Are you sure you're okay? You don't look so good. You wanna skip this and go back to the house?" Tori asked.

"No, babe. I'm fine. Really." I assured her.

Carmen made a snickering noise from within the stall. Lisa said, "Damn homophobic locals. We'll meet you at the entrance, Kenya."

She grabbed Tori's hand walking with and half dragging her out the door. She paused at the door to motion with her head toward Carmen's stall. She winked and then left before Tori noticed anything. I don't know if she knew it was Carmen in there or if she was referring to the 'homophobic local.'

Carmen came out of the stall. "So that was your plan all along, huh? To steal Tori from me. Well you can keep her ass. I got somebody just as good. She might even be better. Fuck the two of yall." She talked big and bad but when she saw me take a menacing step towards her, she took a few steps back.

However, she straightened her spine and continued, "Touch me and I will have my Rasta cousins come to your villa. Then you won't have to worry about your car cause trust me, you won't have hands to drive it. Now get the fuck away from me!"

I was tempted to strangle her right there in the bathroom but I restrained. Instead I told her, "I don't know who the hell you think you are but I'd be careful what kind of threats I issue if I were you."

I left the restroom with my palms sweating and my heart racing. This was all too much for me. I took a few cleansing breaths, trying to get it together before meeting up with the girls. By the time I made it to them, my heart rate was back to normal. I wiped my hands dry, ready for Tori to take hold of it. I plastered on a smile as I walked up to them. Sam seemed relieved that I was back. Guess he was getting impatient.

"Sorry yall. Small bladder today," I said with a fake smile.

They believed me, except for Lisa who lagged back to ask me quietly, "What's going on? You seemed a bit on edge back there."

"Please don't tell Tori."

"I won't. What's wrong?"

I filled her in on the damage to my car, the threatening note, my suspicion of Jewelle, and finally about the run in with Carmen. The other girls were engrossed with Sam's speech about the falls. We climbed the steps with them but every chance we got, we hung back to discuss the situation.

Finally, Tori said, "Babe, I don't know what you and Lisa are whispering about but this is supposed to be a couple's trip. Come here. Please."

I went to her. "I'm sorry," I said, kissing her until the memory of my being distracted left her. The water was cold and I could see her nipples poke through her bikini top. My mouth watered seeing them. Funny how that little sight could clear *my* mind of worries.

Her hands reached down to cup my ass, giving each cheek a squeeze. In the waist deep pool of water on that level of the falls, no one could see what her hands, or fingers, were doing. Her fingers snaked forward and slipped beneath the crotch of my bikini bottom to run alongside my lips. First, outer, then inner, just grazing my clit, making me shudder, before withdrawing deftly. "I have more of that for you later, *if* you're good. Lisa can't do that for you. Remember that," she whispered then gave me a quick peck on the lips and a wink.

I leaned in for another kiss but was interrupted by the sound of Sam clearing his throat noisily. "Although I don't mind the show, I must tell you ladies, some of the people won't like that too much. They don't like people like you," he said.

Lisa said raucously, "In other words, yall need to stop before these HOMOPHOBIC LOCALS get uncomfortable and try to kill us." Toy tried to cover her mouth before she could get all the words out but Lisa's voice rang clear and loud.

Luckily, it was all tourists on that trip up the falls. The only locals were a couple other male guides and they were still at the bottom of the falls. Too far to hear the outburst. A few of the other tourists laughed but Sam did not appreciate the humor.

"Excuse our friend," I told him.

We continued our trek up the waterfall's stone steps, pausing only to snap photos and capture the surroundings on video. At the end, we collected our belongings and thanked Sam for the tour before making our way towards the taxi waiting areas.

We made a quick stop in the market place to buy souvenirs then found our driver. We rode back to the villa, chattering about the falls and what a wonderful experience it was. It wasn't enough to take my mind off the recent developments, but it helped to push it to the back of my mind. I'd worry about those things *after* the vacation.

Tori

The aroma of curried meats greeted us at the door. The owner, Jim, a white man, and his wife, Paulette, were the parents of one of Mik's friends. That's how we were able to get such a good deal on the property. They were pulling plates and glasses out of the cabinets when we arrived.

One meal was provided daily but I had no idea they were the ones preparing it. It was so good, I was sure it was from some expensive, local restaurant. It turns out the family owned a restaurant in town. After introductions, we helped take the food to the patio to eat outside. We invited the couple to stay to eat with us but they had prior engagements.

While eating, we noticed that outdoor furniture, beach chairs, mosquito torches, and string lights were placed on the little sand dune.

"Wow!" Dru exclaimed. "Did you ask them to do that for our evening plans?" she asked Mik.

"No. I haven't said anything to them. I just thought we'd take beach blankets over there. That's amazing."

We verbalized our agreement with full mouths. Just like the day before, we became sleepy after eating. "All this food, we're all going to gain a shit load of weight by the time we go back home. All we do is eat and sleep," Toy said.

We cleaned up the kitchen, putting away the rest of the curried chicken, goat, and shrimp, along with the rice and roasted corn. Not wanting a repeat of the night before, we set our alarms for 3:00 pm as we retired to our sleeping quarters for a brief nap.

In our room, I found myself fighting sleep. It wasn't like me to have this hard of a time staying awake. Full stomach or not. Something just didn't feel right to me. I drifted off to sleep with Kenya's arms around me before I could figure it out.

The sound of the blaring alarm woke me out of deep slumber, with my heart racing. Immediately after, I heard a scream coming from the kitchen. Kenya and I looked at each other, both startled at the sound. We hurried to the kitchen to find Lisa and Toy standing on the kitchen chairs.

Kenya saw what they were looking at, and quickly joined them on a nearby chair. I, being still half asleep, was a bit slower at noticing what frightened them. There was a large, brown, evil–looking iguana lounging in the middle of the kitchen floor. The nearest chair was across the kitchen, meaning I would have to pass the iguana to get to it.

Luckily, Dru and Mik, came running out of their room and scared the critter. It took off running through the open back door. It was about five minutes later when we realized the back door was open. How on earth did it get opened? The six of us were all taking naps. Mik suggested maybe we had left it open in our rush to get to our beds. Kenya seemed a bit unnerved by this theory but she said nothing.

Still feeling groggy from our afternoon nap, we decided to go for a swim. We had been on the island for two days and still had not made it to the beach. The salt water was calling our names. We changed into bathing suits, grabbed beach towels, and headed out the patio door. The sun was out, but there was a soft Caribbean breeze that managed to mask the full effect of it.

Lisa and I looked at each other and immediately knew what the other was thinking. We dropped our towels and ran to Toy, grabbing her by the arms and pulling her into the water. Lisa took it a step further and pulled her feet out from underneath her causing her to fall face first into the water. Boy, was she pissed! She stood up sputtering and wiping at her face before returning the favor to Lisa.

I stood to the side, watching and laughing and did not see Kenya, Dru, and Mik approaching me. By the time I saw them, I was being slammed into the water. I was so caught off guard that I took in a big swallow of the salty water. We played like that for a while, enjoying the carefree moment. Of course, we eventually paired off with Dru and Mik wandering down the beach, Lisa trying to teach Toy how to float, and Kenya and I splashing frivolously in the water.

I pulled Kenya to me, kissing her softly on the lips. Her full lips at first tasted like the salty water we were playing in, but eventually her natural flavors replaced it. We moved to deeper waters, as her hands explored my body from shoulder to thigh and everywhere in between. Her hands fondled my nipples through my bikini top while her thigh slipped between mines to incite me. Our kiss deepened as my hands continued on the path they had begun earlier at the waterfalls.

My fingers caressed her lower lips and played in the crease between her folds. Her soft whimper came through to my lips as a vibration turning me on even more. My middle finger began making circles on her clit as she nibbled on my bottom lip. I could tell the difference between the wetness of the ocean and the wetness of *her* ocean. Hers was slimy but sticky at the same time.

I inserted a finger into the depths of her ocean and heard her purr. Her walls clenched around that solitary finger, begging for more. Now her thigh was between mine and my thigh was between hers as our hips moved on a mind of their own. The motion of the ocean only accentuated the subtle movements.

I have dreamed of having sex in the water, but nothing could prepare me for the intensity of this moment. I could feel my orgasm slowly building and by the crescendo of Kenya's moans, I could tell she was nearing that point as well but I did not want our first time to be a quickie in the water.

I was hoping for something more romantic and longer lasting. I stopped moving my hips and separated our pelvic region just enough for Kenya to get the hint. "Baby, we need to slow down. I don't want our first time to be like this." Kenya groaned her frustration, but I could see the understanding in her eyes. We continued kissing and playing in the water before being joined by the other girls.

We ventured over to the sand dune to check out the small area. It was just large enough for an eight-seater dining table, three lounging chairs, and two hammocks connected each to two palm trees. The Tiki torches held citronella candles to ward off mosquitoes. The setup was perfect.

"This is nice. We can have dinner out here tonight," Dru volunteered.

"I think that was the plan, genius," Lisa responded.

"Toy, control your woman." We all laughed at that one. There was no "controlling" Lisa.

Toy confirmed, "That's between yall. Don't put me in it."

We lounged out on the chairs, relaxed in the hammock, and Dru and Toy even tried climbing the coconut trees. That was a sight to see. I don't think they made it two feet off the ground. When the sun cooled off a good bit, Kenya, Lisa, and Mik, volunteered to go get the food. I offered to help but they insisted I stay out with the bois. Somebody had to keep an eye on them and make sure they didn't drown themselves in knee-high water. I was okay with that. I had found the perfect spot in the hammock.

18

CHAPTER EIGHTEEN

Kenya

Lisa, Mik, and I made sandwiches with a side of chips and lemonade for dinner. The way we had been falling asleep after meals, we didn't need to eat that heavy more than once per day. Besides, I wasn't trying to put on ten pounds during my vacation.

We found a floating tray in the kitchen and used it to float the food over to the sand dune. The bois had taken advantage of the quiet time and were taking another nap.

Being devious, Lisa, Mik, and I took ice cubes from the ice bucket and using our fingers to signal, stealthily put the ice cubes in each of the girls' shorts. Tori was wearing boy shorts so hers was a bit trickier. She felt my hand trying to get under the elastic band at her waist and she grabbed my hands, pulling me down on top of her. That made the hammock flip over, dumping the two of us into the sand. I landed on top of her but she quickly rolled over so she could be on top.

"Now this is how it's supposed to be," she said laughing.

The sexual innuendo was obvious as well as the sexual tension.

"Why don't yall just do it and get it over with? Sheesh!" Toy blurted.

"Whatever. We're taking our time," Tori answered.

Speaking low so only she could hear me, I asked, "When is the right time? Don't you think we've waited long enough?"

"Babe, be easy. We'll know when it's time." She stood before me, helping me to my feet. She dusted off her bathing suit bottom and turned to help put the food on the table. I felt like I was dismissed.

I couldn't help it. I pouted. I wasn't sure what Tori's deal was but I was losing patience. I knew she cared about me but she didn't seem to *want* me. *I'm going to make sure that by the end of this trip, she's not going to be able to walk by me and not want me. I know Lisa said to wait for her to be ready but I'm tired of waiting. This crap ends today!*

My silent monologue ended with Lisa yelling at Toy to get up. "Yall ate too much at lunch. No more of that heavy food. Get your ass up!"

Toy struggled but eventually got to her feet. Dru was already at the table scarffing down her dinner. You'd think she hadn't eaten all day.

"Babe, you're lucky you have a high metabolism cause otherwise, you'd be fat, as much as you eat," said Mik.

Through a mouthful of food, Dru muttered, "Yall femmes always hating."

The dinner conversation was light and playful. We talked about the next day's plans. Toy wanted to go horseback riding and Lisa wanted to get some fish from the market to throw on the grill. Mik suggested we cook the fish island style by wrapping them in banana leaves and cooking them in a hole in the sand. She'd seen it done as a child while visiting her family in Dominica. It was something new and different so we agreed to try it.

When the sky was purple with just a hint of orange from the light of the sun, we loaded up the floating tray and made our way back to the house. A quick clean up of the kitchen, then we retired to our separate quarters to shower and get ready for a night of games. Poker, spades, truth or dare, and of course, some drinking games.

Tori and I jumped in the shower together but neither of us said much. I helped her wash her hair and she helped with mine but there was obvious tension. I was still moody from earlier and too busy in my own thoughts to try at conversation. Tori seemed preoccupied as well. She was out of the shower before I was.

Once I turned the shower off, I could hear soft music playing through the door separating the bedroom from the bathroom. I searched for my clothes I'd laid out on the bathroom counter but they were nowhere in sight. "Tori," I called out to her. There was no answer so I tried a little louder. Still no answer.

I opened the door to the bedroom and was surprised by the setting in front of me. The room was dark except for the faint glow from several candles around the room. The scent of mango and coconut met my nose. Hibiscus flowers were strewn across the floor and onto the bed.

And on the bed, Tori was resting on her side, her dimpled smile framed by her bushy hair. She was waiting patiently for me, as naked as I was beneath my towel. My clothes were tossed onto the couch on the other side of the room. It was all such a pleasant surprise, I didn't move. I couldn't move.

"Come here," she said softly. She patted the spot next to her on the bed. But my feet were planted firmly to the ground. I *wanted* to walk over there, after all, this is the moment I'd been waiting for, but my body wouldn't move.

Tori came to me instead. Her cool fingertips brushed the wet strands of hair from my face. "I was taking my time with you because I wanted this to be special. I've rushed into things with people before and it hasn't lasted. I want us to last.

I love you, Kenya. You've been there for me and when I'm around you, my heart feels light. I get butterflies every time I see you. Electricity flows through me whenever you touch me. You've made friends with my friends and became a part of my family. I'm glad we waited. But if you're still not ready for us to be physical, I don't mind waiting longer."

Those last words were enough to snap me out of my semi-trance. Hell, I wasn't trying to wait any more. I pulled her head to mine and kissed her deeply, hungrily. She responded immediately, kissing me as if I were giving her her oxygen. As if she needed me to subsist.

Her toned arms wrapped around me, pulling me even closer to her. Our bodies intertwined, trying to become just one body. Her warmth burned into me but instead of making me want to pull away from the heat, I yearned to be closer to her.

With just a little force, she pushed me against the bedroom wall, deepening the kiss. Her lips separated from mine to kiss a blazing trail down my neck and across my collarbone. My heart skipped beats as other parts of my body began to throb.

She made her way to my full breasts, taking time to administer attention to each nipple. Her warm tongue bathed them before suckling each one far into her mouth. We moaned at the same time. She kissed her way down my abdomen, dropped to her knees, cupped my ass, and used her tongue to give my clit a tentative lick. At first she lapped at my kitty like a kitten drinking milk. But as my juices began flowing, she drank as if she were thirsty.

With just a slight movement, she hoisted my thighs over her shoulders, having my feet completely off the floor and my back pressed firmly to the wall. She feasted on my pussy until *my* walls convulsed, which lead to the room's walls shaking. Her tongue probed me. Her hands grasped me. I was hers. She could do anything she wanted to me and I wouldn't care. At that moment, she stamped me, *Property of Tori Becker*. I closed my eyes tight, enjoying the sensations reverberating through my body.

My orgasm came out of the blue like a flash of lightning or a massive explosion. I imagined fireworks were going off in my body. A warm, white light encompassed me before I was brought back to reality, only to have another orgasm, and then another, and then another. In all that, my moans and screams pierced the air around us. I'd never been a quiet lover and this time I think I beat my own record. But I didn't care.

I could no longer hear the soft music because her moans matched mine. She'd told me once before that she could orgasm just by pleasuring the other person. She said the sounds, the wetness, and the smell of lovemaking was enough to take her over the edge.

I could no longer feel the cool air because our bodies turned the room into a sauna as sweat formed on our bodies. And the smell of mango and coconut mixed with the scent of our passion to form a unique fragrance only we could create.

Just when I felt like my body couldn't take anymore, Tori allowed my feet to touch the ground, standing straight up to let me sample my juices from her lips and tongue. We kissed, trying to catch our breaths.

There was a knock at the door. Tori called to the visitor, "Yall go on without us." Lisa and Mik laughed, sending whistles and hand claps through the barrier. "Bout damn time!" Lisa yelled.

Sure they were gone, Tori asked, "You good?"

I could only nod. She giggled. "Good. Now I know how to quiet you."

"Whatever," I said, playfully swatting at her.

"Wanna get cleaned up?"

"No. I want to taste you," I answered, pushing her towards the bed. One good shove and she fell backward onto the bed.

"Oh, it's like that?" she asked teasingly. "You're not going to try to top me ----"

Her words were cut off when my arms pulled her ass to the edge of the bed, locking around her thighs and raising them into the air and then spread with her knees to her chest. I dove into her depths as if I were trying to go deep sea diving. I fucked her with my tongue, taking time to collect the juices that were already flowing. Tasting her made me moan with joy. She tasted so ripe and sweet. There just wasn't enough. I wanted more. And I took more.

My hands roamed upward to pull at her nipples while pulling her clit into my mouth. I held it hostage against the roof of my mouth using my lips to suck at the base of it. I hummed a little, letting the vibrations bring her closer and more rapidly to peak. Her body shook when she came, minutes later, her hands pulling at my hair. I didn't mind. Not if it meant she was riding the same wave of orgasms she'd delivered to me.

She pulled me up to lie on her chest. "Wow!" she said. "Wow."

"Don't ever forget that," I said cockily.

"Oh trust, I won't."

We laid like that for a while, enjoying our closeness. But when my fingers reached below to fondle her lower lips, she flipped me onto my back, straddling me. Then, one thigh slipped between mine and she began moving. My wetness spread up and down her thigh with every movement and hers did the same with mine. In sync with one another, we rocked. We rocked while we moaned, and moaned while we came.

The whole time, her eyes never left mine. She called my name as I told her how much I loved her. Our orgasms collided, sending us into a place neither of us had been before. Never had I felt so fulfilled. And when I wiped the tears from my eyes, she mirrored me.

Tori

I knew waiting on Kenya would be worth it but I had no idea it could be so good. When we made love, my mind escaped to a tranquil place. An out of body experience. Whatever you choose to call it, this woman was my perfect match.

She wasn't perfect. She had a blemished past; so did I. But she was perfect for me. And if I wasn't already, I would make sure I was perfect for her. I was planning on putting in my resignation when we returned. I didn't want to, but if the hospital wouldn't allow us to be together, I was going to have to find another job.

It wouldn't be hard. I'd have to give up my condo but I'm sure I could stay with Kenya until I bought us a house. *I'm getting ahead of myself. My first step would be to inform the anesthesia chief and see if he would be okay with keeping me on. After all, I* did *double the size of the department's staff and business. But I'll check out some openings in the area, just in case.*

I was doing all that thinking around two a.m. Kenya shifted positions. I was ready for more. Her back was to me and I started kissing on her neck. She moaned but kept on sleeping. I caressed her butt with one hand and played with her nipple with the other. She wiggled against me and her breathing sped up. I moved a hand to the front to rub her clit. Her pelvis ground against my hand and I could feel her begin to get wet.

"Wait a minute," she said, "be right back."

What the hell? I rolled unto my back, looking up at the ceiling fan. Random thoughts ran through my mind but before I could focus on any one, she was standing at the side of the bed. She had a silly grin on her face and then I saw why. She'd gone to put on a strap. *Oh hell no,* I thought.

"What are you doing?" I asked her.

"Having fun. Why? Something wrong?"

"Ummmm, sweetie, I don't do penetration. I mean, I can penetrate you, but I don't get penetrated."

"There's a first time for every thing, right? Come on," she pleaded.

I laid on my back looking at the ceiling fan again. I closed my eyes. Penetration was a no-no for me. But I'm here thinking about quitting my job for this woman so surely I could . . . *Ugh!*

"Ok, but please, be gentle. The biggest thing I've had in there is a tampon."

She laughed. She tried to calm my nerves by distracting me with gentle kisses. That didn't work -- until those kisses moved down my body stopping at my inner thighs. Her mouth worked its magic, bringing me to ecstasy in just a few minutes. She turned me onto my stomach and repeated from the back. It was amazing. Again, I came within minutes. Just as the second orgasm was subsiding, she inserted the dildo, an inch at first. I felt myself trying to tense up and so did she.

"Relax, baby," she whispered in my ear, nibbling on my lobe as she did so. Her fingers reached around to my front to massage my clit. My walls relaxed enough for her to penetrate me fully. The feeling of fullness was actually pleasant. It didn't feel like hard plastic. It was actually soft.

She moved gently at first, building up a rhythm, her hand never leaving my clit. Her pace picked up, keeping time with my heart. She moaned as I gasped, screamed and squealed. Our bodies made a musical beat as we rocked our way to simultaneous orgasms.

"Damn, BABY!" I screamed as the last wave shook my body. She sucked at the flesh on my back, caressing my ass until she pulled out and collapsed on the bed. We panted. Sex could be such a workout.

The sun was shining bright into the room when we were awakened by knocks on our door. "Get yall asses up! We got horses to ride." Dru called out.

If only she knew we'd been riding all night.

The next few days felt like a honeymoon, except with friends. Kenya and I made love every night and took advantage of daytime hours of freedom as well. No place that afforded even a small amount of privacy was excluded. The beach. Late night out on the sand dune. In the pool. Down the private beach. And multiple times in the hot tub. You'd think we were trying make up for lost time. I was glad our sexual appetites matched each other. You remember that Destiny's Child lyric, "tap me on my shoulder I'll roll over"? That was Kenya. I'd hit the jackpot.

Then there were all the activities that we did as a group. We did the horseback riding tour. That was fun. The tour ended with a ride on the beach and in the water. We rode jet skis. Or, *we* rode. Dru and Toy held on for their lives and screamed like little girls. It was so funny, some of the locals gathered on the beach to laugh at them.

We snorkeled in a small reef Mik and Dru found on one of their alone time excursions at the far end of the beach. We saw sea anemone, starfish, different sizes, colors, and species of fish, some sea urchins, and a few jellyfish. Spotting the jellyfish ended our little adventure.

Toy, Mik, and Dru bought some special "herbs" for some of their extracurricular activities. Kenya and I don't smoke so we opted out. And since Lisa was taking hormones to prepare for in vitro fertilization once we got back to Atlanta, she passed as well. Those three crazy women puffed on that magic dragon and acted the damn ass. We made sure to capture it on video for blackmailing purposes at a later date.

We had a great vacation. But strangely, I was ready to go home. I had some business to tend to. Namely, knocking out the obstacles that try to keep Kenya and I from each other.

19

CHAPTER NINETEEN

Kenya

I was beginning to believe we were being followed. It was just a feeling I had whenever we left the property. In the last few days, we've been horseback riding, snorkeling, jet skiing, and today we were shopping in the market. I kept looking over my shoulders. At one point, I thought I saw Jewelle but when I walked over to the booth where I though I saw her, she was not there. I mentioned this to Lisa who said she'd keep and eye out but we never saw her again.

At the market, we bought lots of souvenirs, some rum cakes, and a few bottles of liquor. It was our last full day on the island and our plan was to get toasted before we flew out that next morning.

When we got back to the house, we found the front door mat moved off to the side. Almost as if someone were looking for the key. They wouldn't have had much luck though, because we had that key with us. "Must be some locals thinking they could steal our stuff," Toy theorized.

"Well they ought to be slapped for that shit. They better be glad they didn't get in because I woulda had to put a bullet in their ass," Dru said.

"You brought your gun?" asked Mik.

"No, but I got one from one of the locals that day we went horseback riding."

"I thought you were buying smoke. What if you bought a dirty gun?" Mik was freaking out. I think I was too. Tori, Toy, and Lisa seemed unfazed.

"Safety first. Besides, it's not like they trace that shit anyway. This is Jamaica 'mon'. Don't worry, be happy," she said in her best Jamaican accent which really wasn't that good.

"I don't like that, Dru."

"Like I said, safety first."

I pulled Tori over to the side. "Why did Dru buy a gun? Do you think we're in danger?"

"Kenya, it's like she said. We just have it for security. Don't stress about it. Okay?"

She gave me a quick peck before walking to the kitchen where the others were cracking open Red Stripes. We spent the rest of the afternoon drinking and lounging on the beach.

I needed time to talk to the girls. While warming the food, I recapped all that had been going on within the last couple of weeks. Mik seemed surprised but, then again, I guess she would be. She wasn't around when most of the drama took place. She hadn't heard about the car break in.

She also hadn't heard about Jewelle and Maria. But she was extremely flustered when I told her about Carmen and Tori. She asked me to describe Carmen. When I did, she burst into tears. Lisa and I were confused as to what was going on. We tried to console her but at the same time, we were trying to figure out what caused her to be so upset. This is where things get sticky.

"Carmen is the friend that recommended this place to me."

"What!?!?" Lisa and I exclaimed at the same time.

"I didn't know. I was wondering why she was

encouraging me to get to know Dru. At the forum during Pride, where I met you guys, she was with me," she said to me.

"I don't remember seeing her."

"She saw Dru stand up during the discussion and suggested I go talk to her. After the forum, I did, but when I went back to where we were all standing, the other girls said she had left. We still hang out from time to time and she knows I'm with Dru now. When I mentioned that you guys wanted to go on a vacation, she suggested her parents place. That's when I told Lisa about it."

"Well fuck, if I had known the devil's parents owned this place, I would have said 'Hell no!'" said Lisa.

"Well, if I had known she was the devil, I wouldn't have told you about it. I really am sorry. I had no idea."

"I saw her the other day at the Falls," I told Mik.

"Who? Carmen? What is she doing here?"

"She said she is visiting with some friends."

"Oh yea, she did say she was planning a trip with these girls she met at the Pride picnic. Just didn't think it would be so soon. That's another weird story."

"Oh yea? What?" Lisa asked.

"Well, she said she met this couple at the picnic. Like a *real* couple. A relationship couple. But they invited her to their house. She went and got turned out I think. Now, they are all serious and shit. Like, the more aggressive one asked her to move in with them. Crazy shit like that."

Immediately, I knew she was talking about Jewelle and Maria. I described them to her and she confirmed. It was them. Guess they'd found their third party. When you think about it, that might be the ideal situation for them.

Our conversation was interrupted by a knock at the door.

Tori

"Dru, you shouldn't have mentioned that gun, man. Now you got Mik and Kenya all freaked out," I said to her. The three of us -- Dru, Toy, and I -- were sitting out on the sand dune while the girls were preparing dinner. We'd asked the owners to stop bringing food because I couldn't figure out why we all got so sleepy after meals. I didn't know if we were being drugged or if they cooked with something that really cause severe postprandial somnolence

(AKA: niggeritis or the –itis), but since we've been cooking for ourselves, we've been more like ourselves.

"Shit, I'm sorry. But what yall think of the doormat? And what about that iguana that got into the house? How did it get in if all the windows and doors were closed and locked? I'm telling you, something isn't right."

"I'm with Dru, Tori," Toy added. "The girls needed to know what's going on. What if something were to pop off? They'd be completely caught off guard. And sorry to say it but that little chic you messed with seems damn conniving and malicious."

I sat quietly, listening. I knew they were right. I'd been extra guarded since spotting Carmen at the horse stables when we went riding. It might have been just a coincidence, but then I saw Jewelle at the market a few hours later. And she was talking to Carmen. I didn't know how they knew each other, but the two women who would be most resolute about ruining our lives, were here at the same time, in another country. That and the phone calls and the vandalism to our cars, were a bit much. Lisa had given me heads up on what happened to Kenya's car. Kenya still wasn't aware that I knew.

"Okay, okay. Good thing we're leaving tomorrow. And other than those couple incidents, it's been an uneventful trip." As soon as the words were out of my mouth, there was a loud commotion from inside the house and a scream that made my hairs stand on end.

Without hesitation, the three of us raced through the water as fast as we could, leaving the setting sun behind us.

Toy was first at the door and as she burst in, a shot rang out, hitting her in the upper arm. She screamed in pain before hitting the floor. Panic ensued. I was right behind her and Dru right behind me. I caught Toy's head before it could come in contact with the ground. Lisa, Kenya, and Mik were screaming and crying.

Behind them stood Carmen and Jewelle. They too were screaming. I couldn't understand was going on. My mind tried to focus but Toy's screams distracted me. That and the blood. There was a lot of blood. I guessed the bullet hit the brachial artery in her arm.

"SHUT THE FUCK UP! SHUT UP! Or somebody else is going to get shot!" the slightly familiar voice yelled. I looked up and there stood Skye. She held two guns, one pointed at the girls and one pointed at the door where I was bent over holding pressure on Toy's wound.

"Please let me help her," Lisa pleaded, with tears pouring down her face.

She seemed to think about it then answered, "Go ahead but try anything and she'll get another one. In the meanwhile, bitch, get your ass over here next to your little trick!" she said that part to me.

I wanted to defy her but I knew my friends' lives were in danger. This girl was obviously crazy. So instead of telling her how much I wanted to hurt her, I said, "Let her come over here first and hold the wound. Then I'll let go." When she nodded, I said to Lisa, "Come on, Lis."

Lisa released Kenya's hand. She was on one side of Kenya and Mik was on the other. Behind them, Carmen and Jewelle were also holding hands. Toy's screams lessened to quiet sobs, the initial shock of it all, wearing off. Lisa came to her and I showed her where to compress the artery to prevent any more bleeding. I pulled the drawstring out of the waist of my cargo shorts, tying a tourniquet above the bullet's entrance.

"Hurry up, bitch! Get your ass over here with your ho ass girlfriend."

I walked to Kenya, never turning my back to Skye, with both hands raised. Kenya's hand, moist with nervous sweat, grabbed mine in a vice like grip. She was shaking. I reached to wipe the tears from her face. That really pissed Skye off. She fired a shot to the area just left of my shoulder. I know she wasn't trying to hit me. She just wanted to scare me. It worked. *I got to get us out of this. But how?*

Out of the corner of my eye, I saw Dru creep off the back porch. Skye hadn't spotted her and obviously didn't know she was out there. *Please go get help, Dru,* I thought to myself. Since we'd been out in the water, we didn't have any cell phones with us but maybe she could run to the street and flag down help. Or so I hoped.

Skye spoke, her voice laced with hatred. "I came here for you, doc. You think you could embarrass me like that in front of all those people and get away with it. I am Rainbow Skye. YOU DON'T FUCK WITH ME! And then you try to steal my woman."

"I am NOT your woman! We broke up years ago." Kenya's voice was shaky but her voice let her know she wasn't going down without a fight.

"Oh really? How about I shoot your damn doctor friend here and we'll see what you think about it then?" She waved the gun wildly around as she spoke. Carmen and Jewelle screamed and ducked behind us. Lisa's sobs grew louder and Kenya's grip tightened on my hand.

"Skye, you came for me. Let the others go. Toy is hurt. These people have done nothing to you," I said. I sounded like one of those brave people you see in the movies but really, I was about to shit my pants. The way I saw it, if they could get out, maybe Dru would be back with help by then. That way, if she shot me, the cops could take her down and hopefully the paramedics could save me. Either way, it was obvious this girl was going to try to kill me. Why let the others get hurt as well?

Kenya wasn't too happy with me. She jerked me around to face her, "Hell no! It's me she wants. I'll go with her."

"No, she'll kill you."

"YALL SHUT THE FUCK UP! You think this is open to discussion? I have the gun. I say who dies. Nobody is going anywhere."

She began pacing the room. From her pensive expression, I gathered she had not bargained on all of us being here. She probably thought it was just Kenya and I on vacation here. Shit, I was still trying to decipher how Carmen and Jewelle got here. How did they fit into this?

20

CHAPTER TWENTY

Kenya

When we heard the knock on the door earlier, we kicked into survival mode. Lisa and I grabbed kitchen knives, ready to defend ourselves as needed, and Mik went to open the door. In retrospect, one of us should have notified Tori, Dru, and Toy.

On the other side of the door, stood Carmen and Jewelle. I would have been totally surprised had we not just had that conversation about them being here. However, *they* seemed surprise at our lack of surprise. Or maybe it was because we had knives pointed at them.

"What the hell? Can I get a hello?" Jewelle said smartly.

"Uh, hell no! What do you want Jewelle? Yall have caused enough trouble."

Carmen, who'd been as still as a statue, finally spoke. "We don't like you but we haven't done anything to you."

"Well, actually, we have," Jewelle corrected her, "But that's why we're here. Can we talk? Please."

Lisa gave me a nod of agreement. I allowed the two she devils into the house and led them to the living room.

"You can sit," Lisa told them. They looked nervous about doing so but they did.

"Talk," Lisa ordered.

Jewelle spoke. "Okay, first let me say, I am so sorry. I am not very good with rejection and I think I might have taken things too far."

"Ya think?!" I interrupted. "You sent me a death threat. Messed up our cars. You're following us on our vacation."

"That's some straight up, psycho shit!" Lisa added.

"And you betrayed my trust," Mik said to Carmen.

"We didn't send any death threats. And although Carmen did mention to us that she wanted to get you back for hitting her, we didn't trash your cars. As far as following you here, we were just trying to warn you."

"Warn me about what? And if that's the truth, why didn't Carmen 'warn' me when she saw me at the falls?" I asked.

"I was going to tell you but then you got to running your mouth and it pissed me off. You wouldn't have believed me anyway."

"You're right. Continue, Jewelle."

"So when Carmen told me about you, she was still working at AGH. She told me you were trying to steal Tori from her. . ." When she saw me open my mouth to disagree with her, she held up her hand to stop me. "Let me finish. We have to hurry so we can get out of here. Anyway, she told me about how you dated Skye in the past. I knew Skye well. We'd been friends for quite some time. I set it up for Skye to come back into your life. That was what happened at the party. I was okay with taking you out of the picture myself by having you in my life, but you rejected the idea.

Things got out of hand. When Tori punched Skye it shook her up. She's used to being in control and that was a blow to her ego. So when Carmen mentioned that you hit her at Strokers, the three of us got together to find a way to get back at you. Carmen wanted me to leak the video I made of us to Tori's practice members. That was fine with me. But Skye didn't feel like that was enough. She talked about fucking up your cars, poisoning you, scaring you by issuing anonymous threats, killing you, even. We didn't think she had it in her to truly do any damage. Either way, that was way above our vengeance scale. And she said she would keep it simple."

I sat in stunned silence. Mik was crying and Lisa was pacing the floor nervously. The story was unbelievable but believable at the same time.

With a cue from Jewelle, Carmen continued the story. "I saw you guys at the forum that Sunday. I amped Mik up to go talk to Dru. By the way, I'm sorry for using you, Mik. I really am. My idea was to get Mik to tell us what was going on with you and Tori."

She continued on to tell us how Skye tried to persuade them to do more. They'd refused and she stopped speaking to them. Then she came back around while Tori was hospitalized.

"I had Mik on speakerphone when she asked about my parent's beach house being available. She overheard and started talking about being overdue for a vacation. She seemed to be over her desire for revenge but we needed to tag along and talk her out of whatever crazy shit she planned to do.

It started as a nice vacation but she disappeared that first day you got here. I thought she was at the house but when I got here, she was not. I didn't think anything of it until my dad said he found a strange bottle of medicine in his kitchen trash at the restaurant. She'd helped out that day and apparently spiked the food with a sleeping medicine.

We confronted her about it. Told her she was jeopardizing her career *and* ours. She said it was just a simple practical joke. She also told us she'd planted a camera in all the bedrooms. She's sent those videos to the hospital. I'm so sorry."

"Oh my God! My career is over," I said before bursting into tears.

"Kenya, I don't like how things went between us and I am so sorry," said Jewelle. "I've asked a friend of mine to intercept the mail. He works in the mailroom there. That's the least I could do, considering."

That slowed the tears but I knew more were coming.

Jewelle continued, "She wants revenge. I don't know exactly what she has planned but she's been acting really strange the last two days. I think she's lost it, for real. I know you guys aren't leaving till tomorrow but you should leave tonight. Like right now!"

I could hear the panic in her voice. Lisa and Mik looked terrified. "Get Tori, Dru, and Toy, NOW!" I ordered. They were headed to the back door when the front door was kicked in.

Skye stood menacingly in the doorway, wearing casual jeans and a Jamaican "Don't worry, be happy" t-shirt, but there was nothing happy about her. Her eyes shot wildly around the room. Surprise was evident on her face once it registered how many of us there were in the room. I think she had planned on it being just Tori and I. Instead, it was five women against just her.

Carmen reached for her purse next to her. Skye saw the slight movement and yelled, "Hand it over here Carmen. The whole purse."

Carmen did as she was told. Skye pulled out a small gun, laughing as she did so. "Thanks, Carmen. I'm going to need this since the number or participants has grown." She pointed the two guns at us. Ordering us to the kitchen area.

"Where's your little friend, Kenya?" she asked.

I didn't answer.

"You always were a little defiant bitch. That's okay though, I got something for your ass." Mik was the closest one to her so she became her punching bag. With one hand she slapped Mik across the face with the gun and with the other hand, she pointed the other gun in my face. We all screamed as Mik fell backward into the barstool causing it to hit the floor with a loud crash.

"Please, don't hurt her," I pleaded, tears blinding me. "What do you want? *You* broke up with *me* years ago."

"I don't care. You are *MINE*," she yelled. "I never stopped loving you. I tried to find you for years. Then, when I do see you again, you had the nerve to disrespect me in front of your little friend and all those people at the club. And that bitch hit me!"

"She was defending me."

"SHUT THE FUCK UP!"

The room was quiet for just a couple seconds until Toy burst through the patio door. It all happened so suddenly, I think Skye was caught off guard and she fired the gun without even taking time to aim.

Luckily for Toy, it was too low and too far to the left so it ended up in her right arm. It could have been her head. Tori's stunned face was visible once Toy crumpled to the ground in pain and shock. I saw Dru take cover behind the wood decking but Skye didn't act like she saw her. Instead, she focused on Tori.

Tori

Skye had lost her damn mind. She kept wiping invisible sweat from her forehead, each time waving the gun carelessly. I glanced over at Toy. She was still losing blood but Lisa had firm pressure over the wound, minimizing the loss. Her dark skin looked slightly gray from the shock of it all. We had to get her some help.

As if the Man above heard me, I saw Dru behind Skye, slip from one side of the hallway to another. She'd entered Toy and Lisa's bedroom through one of the windows and was creeping down the hall to her own room. Probably to get the gun she'd hid in her dresser drawer. Kenya squeezed my hand hard. She'd also seen Dru. Mik gasped. Yep, she'd spotted her too.

Skye realized something was going on and she whipped her head around to see what it was. In that split second, I yanked my hand away from Kenya as she screamed, "NOOOOOOO." But I was already across the room.

I bent at the knees, allowing the force of my shoulders to accost Skye's legs. She was caught by surprise. The two guns exploded as she pulled the trigger, falling backward to the floor. I heard loud screams as I felt a sting across the left side of my head. My world faded to black as the sound of three loud pops echoed.

21

CHAPTER TWENTY-ONE

Kenya

When Tori slammed into Skye, it knocked Skye off balance. As she fell backward to the floor, both guns went off. One bullet hit Tori causing blood to seep from the side of her head. The other bullet hit one of the windows.

Simultaneously, Carmen grabbed a gun from the waistband at her back. She made it to Skye just as she aimed the gun at Tori's unconscious body. Seeing Carmen, Skye quickly took a shot just barely grazing Carmen's leg. In that instant Carmen pointed and fired hitting Skye in the abdomen and Dru emerged, firing the final shot to Skye's head.

It all happened so rapidly, it was easy to believe it had all been a dream. A nightmare. Except for the blood. That was real. As was the screams, sobs, crying, and yelling. Total chaos had invaded our lives in the span of fifteen minutes. Or at least that's what the policeman put in his report.

Jewelle had called the police on her phone, keeping it in her purse during the whole encounter. While I thought they were 'cowering' behind us, it turns out they were using that opportunity to not only call the police but for Carmen to take a gun from Jewelle's purse and hide it in the waist of her pants.

Dru made it to her room, grabbed the gun, and raced back to the living room in time to see Skye take aim at Tori. Although Carmen's shot could have been fatal, it was Dru's gun that fired the kill shot.

As Tori, Toy, and Carmen were raced to the hospital, the police retained the rest of us for questioning at the house. I fought to go with Tori, but they wouldn't allow it. They assured me hers was a surface wound. It nicked the temporal artery making it bleed severely but it wasn't as bad as it looked. She blacked out because of the same reason. Apparently, a punch to the same area would be sufficient to knock someone out.

The police asked a lot of questions about how the guns were acquired. We told them the truth. Some of their eyes showed disdain for "our kind" but others were sympathetic to our plight. They were going to arrest Dru, Carmen, and Jewelle for possession of illegal firearms but Carmen's uncle was chief of police and managed to work some things out. We were finally able to go to the hospital.

Carmen received stitches in the emergency room so by the time we made it to the hospital she was waiting for us at the main entrance. She and Jewelle hugged and kissed passionately. As weird as their relationship was, it worked for them. Together, the six of us rode the elevator to the ICU in complete silence.

There were only semi-private rooms so Toy and Tori shared the small room. Lisa, Mik, and Dru ran to Toy first. She was wide-awake but had several wires hooked to her. She was receiving a unit of blood to replace what she'd lost earlier. There was a second unit hanging, waiting to be transfused. She groaned as she hugged Lisa but still pulled her close. Theirs was real love.

I slowly pulled back the curtain separating Toy and Tori. I was scared of what she must look like. She was sleeping peacefully. The white surgical bandages wrapped around her head like a turban. Luckily, she didn't require oxygen and her wound only needed a few stitches.

"She's been sleeping since we got here. They gave her some pain medicine on the ride over when she woke up screaming. Think she was freaking out because she didn't know what had happened to you. She's been good since though." Toy tried her best to make me feel better but I couldn't help but feel guilty.

"I should have told her about the threat and the busted up windows in my car. I can't believe Skye was behind all that." Sobs tore through my body. Carmen and Jewelle, of all people, came over to console me. Mik and Dru sent looks of sympathy my way.

But it was Lisa who told me, "She knew. I told her. To her, you are worth the risk. She's planning on telling her boss about your relationship, too. Tori decided you were worth the sacrifice. Even when she got the threatening phone call, she was determined not to give up on what you two have."

"What threatening phone call?" I asked.

Dru answered, "That Friday before we came she got a call warning her to stay away from you. She didn't want you to worry."

"And I didn't want *her* to worry. We could have avoided all this."

"How? The only way you could have stopped this was to stop loving each other. Could you have done that?" Toy asked.

"No," I answered immediately. "I love her too much. But we could have pretended. . ."

Carmen cut in, "No you couldn't. It shows all over you. It has since that first day I saw you with her."

"You can't hide true love," Jewelle continued.

"So now what? If she tells the anesthesia group about us, she'll lose her job. She's worked so hard to get where she is now."

"If it came down to that, she can find another job. It won't be hard at all. It might not pay as much or have as many fringe benefits, but what is a sacrifice if by giving it up, you gain everything you ever wanted in life? She loves you that much. This isn't a fling for her. You're it." Lisa's words made my heart feel less heavy. But as I looked down on Tori, the sobs started up again.

"I don't want her to lose her job though. I'll quit my fellowship and find a job somewhere else."

Tori stirred and was barely able to mumble, "Your ass better not quit."

"Tori," everyone rushed to her bed but she focused on me. "You will finish your fellowship. If anybody has to leave, it will be me. You *need* to finish. But let me see what they say when I tell them."

"Okay, baby." I kissed her dry lips. "How's your head?"

"It's good. What happened?"

The sea of voices, filled with emotion, blended with the bleeps of the heart monitor as we told her the whole story.

22

CHAPTER TWENTY-TWO

Kenya

The eight of us flew back on the same flight to Atlanta two days later. Maria greeted us at the airport. Her, Carmen, and Jewelle left before the bags even arrived. They were anxious to begin their life together. Carmen was moving into the house the following weekend and Maria had finally moved in while they were in Jamaica.

Kenya's parents showed up around five minutes later and brought my parents along to surprise me. They'd been informed of the drama but assured by Kenya's father, that all was well. And it was. All I had was a surface wound. Poor Toy was the one who was really hurt. The bullet hadn't hit any nerves though, so she shouldn't need physical therapy. Even if she did, she had Lisa, now the Director of Rehabilitation for the Atlanta Talons NFL team.

News of Skye's death spread quickly around Atlanta. It reported her as an innocent victim of gang violence while visiting friends in Jamaica. It was quite the cover-up. Meanwhile, Kenya and I stated that we simply needed more vacation time.

Since my hair and scrub cap easily covered my wound, I returned to work that Friday morning. Kenya was a nervous wreck, and I guess I kinda was too. I was going to inform the boss of our relationship. Better he heard from me before a video did manage to slip through the mail and onto his desk. I was so nervous, that when Kenya's dad offered to come with us for moral support, I agreed without hesitation.

After my first case, the three of us met Dr. Smith in his office. He knew I was coming but didn't know why. Having the two Dr. Jacksons along only made him more confused.

"Please, have a seat," he said after proper greetings. "To what do I owe this visit?"

I took a deep breath before barging into the conversation. Better to just say it and get it over with. Right? "Sir, I am so sorry. We have violated hospital policy. . ."

Dr. Jackson didn't particularly like my choice of words. He interrupted, "Look William, these two women are both adults. Tori here, has been the driving force in the expansion of your pain service. Your patient load has grown to the point where you needed to hire three staff members and two extra nurses. That is beyond amazing!

My Kenya has made great strides in pediatric surgery. Especially now that she has her pain management certification under her belt. Both departments are blessed to have them. Now I know what the hospital policy is regarding the fraternization of trainee and attending, but these women are in love. And I am telling you right now, if either of them has to go, then I will be going as well. It is time we learn to look the other way for a change. I never took you for a stickler for rules."

I sat back, mouth wide open, my hand gripping the arms of my chair. Kenya's legs were shaking so bad, it made my chair vibrate as well. That was so not helping my already bubbly tummy.

"Phillip, you don't think I already knew that?" Our stunned faces gave him his answer. He laughed boisterously. "We all saw it. The policy was put into place to prevent abuse of power or trainees using sexual favors to get ahead. That was obviously not the case with Dr. Becker and Kenyatta. Besides, Dr. Jackson is no longer a trainee under the anesthesia department so we feel comfortable in looking the other way. Now, I wouldn't go around broadcasting it to the rest of the hospital. Lay low. Do like the military. We won't ask you. You don't tell us. Okay?"

"Yes sir!" Kenya and I chorused. She gave my hand a joyful squeeze.

"Thank you, William." Dr. Jackson added.

"Now, please get out of here. People might think I'm in trouble or something," he joked.

We thanked him again before leaving. Our moods were much brighter than when we came just a few minutes ago.

Later that evening, we were having dinner at Kenya's parent's house. My parents had already left for Houston so it was just the four of us. Kenya's father was replaying the meeting with Dr. Smith. He exaggerated his role a bit but Kenya and I let him have it. No need in dulling his shine. Her mother was pleased with the group's decision to look the other way. I was too. Although I would have done it if I had to, I am glad I did not have to find another job.

Then Kenya announced, "I think we should move in together."

Her father choked on his baked chicken, coughing violently. Her mother handed him his glass of water, calmly, and said, "I think that's a great idea."

They all looked to me for my reaction. It's not that I thought it was a bad idea, but still, I wasn't sure.

"Don't say no just yet, Tori," Kenya said seeing the doubtful expression my face must have bared. I never was good at hiding my feelings.

She continued, "We live next door to each other. We'll spend every night together at either your place or mine anyway. And Dru has been looking for someplace bigger to live now that her and Mik are moving in together. She could stay at your place. And you can come to mine. Then if us living together doesn't work out, you can still go back to your loft."

"I think we'll live fine together. That's not what I'm worried about. Let me think on it."

Kenya's mom tried to sweeten the deal. "Well, while you're thinking, the tenants are moving out of the penthouse condo at the end of the month. We haven't been able to find anyone looking for a four-bedroom condo, especially at that price range, but we have a few looking for a two bedroom. Maybe you two can take the penthouse. That's if you decide you love my daughter enough to put up with her obsessive compulsive ways, Tori."

"What?!!" Kenya, her father, and I echoed. Followed by a chorus of, "Mom, that would be great!" "Honey are you sure?" and "Wow!"

"Tori, think about it. No pressure," Mrs. Jackson added before turning her attention back to her meal.

"Yes, ma'am," I answered. I already knew what my answer would be. My decision wasn't swayed by the large, penthouse condo. I would live with Kenya because I knew she was the woman I wanted to spend my life with. Even if we lived in a one-bedroom apartment, I wouldn't care. As long as I shared it with her.

We moved into the penthouse loft a month later. It was early November. The leaves were just starting to leave their place in the trees. Maybe it was metaphoric of our leaving our separate places and settling together in one place. For the leaves, it was the ground. For us, it was a four bedroom, four and a half bathroom, two-story penthouse with views of the Atlanta skyline.

It had only been five months since I'd met Kenya but the relationship we'd built and the obstacles we'd overcome, made it seem longer. Some might say we did a 'U-Haul,' but time can be subjective. What I had with Kenya was more that I'd had with all my relationships combined. This woman proved that she was willing to make major sacrifices for me. We'd been put to the test and we passed it with flying colors. We were claiming our chance at love.

EPILOGUE

I hear the birds chirping and cars driving by. The sunlight is arranged across my bed in streaky patterns through the cracks of the custom wood blinds. *Why on earth did I decide to live in the city with all this vehicular and foot traffic?* Even from this high, I could hear the city come to life. Even through the closed window I could smell fresh cinnamon rolls and cookies being made in the bakery across the street. *Ugh! It's too early in the morning.*

The sheets next to me rustle and my legs are caressed by soft long legs as the creature sharing my space stirs. I pretend to be still asleep as I feel her prop up on her elbow, watching me. Her finger lovingly traces my face from my ear, to my jaw line, to the outline of my lips. Still pretending, I whimper softly, licking my lips, in my 'sleep'. This encourages her. I feel the bed shifting and my heart picks up speed. Her moist lips connect with mine. Still 'sleeping,' I whisper incoherently and turn my head slightly towards the window, away from her.

She laughs and says, "Girl, get up. I know you are *not* sleeping. We both know you wouldn't turn your head towards that window with all that sunlight coming in like that. First thing we need to do today is get some dark drapes to block that sun out your eye in the morning. Then we need to unpack some of these boxes and do some grocery shopping. And you know the girls are coming this afternoon . . ."

Her next words were muffled as I kissed her firmly and passionately, claiming her lips as mine. I was sitting straight up, watching patiently as she spoke, each word, causing her pink tongue to call to me. I couldn't resist any longer. I had to kiss her.

I feel her heart beat increase in speed and intensity as she straddles me. The beat of her heart, matching the beat of mine. I grab her long dark brown hair and massage her scalp with my fingers. She loves when I do that. I feel her grinding her pelvis against mine as she tries to ease the fire we've ignited.

"Slow down baby," I whisper as I reluctantly break the kiss. I flip her over on her back and straddle her. My hands caress her breasts as my lips and tongue make licking and sucking motions across her neck and lips. They make the journey following my hands, down to her breast, across her flat stomach, down one thigh, and up the next. She shudders as I near her hot spot.

Her moans and whimpers drown out the sounds of the birds. Her sweet scent eliminates the smells of the bakery across the street. And the vision of her anticipatory facial expression, makes me forget about the sunlight that was annoying me minutes ago. Now that sunlight is my friend as it bathes across her beautiful caramel brown skin and face.

Unable to hold out any longer, I dive in to feast on her. Her sweet nectar flows over my lips and drowns my tongue. She grinds her pussy into my face when my tongue flicks over her clit and my lips suck at it's base.

She grabs my hairs, pulling me in closer, as it that was even possible. My face had already become one with her jukebox as my mouth danced to the rhythm it played. She yells my name, "TORI, TORI. OH SHIT. FUCK ME. DAMN BABY. FUCK ME."

I can't help but giggle. She talks so nasty when I'm fucking that pussy. "YOU LIKE THAT BABE? YOU LIKE THAT?"

"SHUT UP AND FUCK ME!"

I laugh again, this time using the vibrations from it to take her higher. I look up at her face in time to see her eyes roll back and her face morph into an ugly-pretty expression.

When the last wave of orgasms subsides, I kiss her, letting her taste her sweetness from my tongue. We hold each other, catching our breaths. "Damn baby," she said breathlessly, "you are worth every sacrifice." I laugh as she drifts off to sleep.